Miss Bennett's Naughty Secret

A Scandal in Surrey novel

Sandra Sookoo

Adventure, Humor, Inclusion, Romance

New Independence Books

MISS BENNETT'S NAUGHTY SECRET ©2013 by Sandra Sookoo
Published by New Independence Books and Sandra Sookoo
Digital ISBN- 9781507082454
Print ISBN- 9798201879853
Contact Information:
sandrasookoo@yahoo.com
newindependencebooks@gmail.com
Visit me at sandrasookoo.com
Book Cover Design by Sandra Sookoo
Stock photo: Deposit Photos
Publishing History
Second Digital Edition, 2016
Third Digital Edition, 2022
First Print Edition, 2022

Blurb

She wants security... Miss Elinor Bennett—an American transplant to England—is at her wit's end. Alone and abandoned following the deaths of her parents and brother in unrelated accidents, her only means of escape from sadness is spying on the new neighbor—and allowing her fingers to wander.

He wants respect... Geoffrey Ansley, bastard son of an earl, has just inherited real estate in Surrey. A solicitor by trade and half-American by birth, he hopes his past won't follow him. Discovering the pretty redhead next door shares his adopted country is a happy accident. And though he wishes to be left alone, he can't banish his neighbor from his mind—especially after he catches her in a secret passage just outside his bedroom one night.

Sometimes fate is a fickle mistress... When a Guy Fawkes prank threatens to expose Elinor's penchant for scandalous exploits and puts Geoffrey's much valued reputation into jeopardy, they will need to decide what's more important—staying one step ahead of the rumor mongers or falling in love no matter the cost.

Dedication

To every reader who has enjoyed the Scandal in Surrey series, and to all the readers who will read the books in the future. I loved writing them for you.

Author's Note

While this story is set at the end of the Regency time period, I'm of the opinion that both men and women in this era had the ability for forward thinking and could have shown this in their actions as well. No one ever moves forward unless the status quo is challenged.

As such, I have taken a bit of literary license with my characters and the world in which they reside in the hopes that it will bring this period to life with a bit of different perspective. The fact these characters are completely naughty and not regretful of their behavior lends another level to the genre. It doesn't mean they're not "real" Regency stories, it merely means they're a different brand of stories.

Chapter One

Late May, 1820, Guildford Surrey

No, no, no!

"I refuse to believe you're moving away," Miss Elinor Bennett lamented to her friend, Beatrice Forsythe. Though the other woman was a few years younger, they'd been fast friends ever since they met at the manse ten years before when Elinor's parents had died. She clasped the other woman's hand. "I'll miss you very much." Beatrice had kept her anchored in sanity after that fatal carriage ride, and if it hadn't been for her friend, she'd be in Bedlam for certain. In order to hide her misty eyes, Elinor glanced out the parlor window. It was raining outside, dismal to match her mood, and in the distance, the gray roof of her manor house beckoned over the tree tops.

"Don't be sad, Ellie. I'm only going to London. We shall see each other often." Beatrice patted Elinor's hand. "William is a wonderful man." A smile beamed from her face. "I promise to write every day, you'll come to Town for the wedding, and you'll be the first person I tell if I'm with child."

Elinor nodded. Her friend had become engaged three months before, ever closer to her living her fondest wish of having a handful of children. "I shall be lonely without you.

Who will I talk to? What will I do?" Now that Beatrice was leaving, Elinor would truly be alone.

"Pish posh. You have family here."

"Not close family. I've long since forgotten the history of how my uncle came to own this property, and besides, my cousin is a terror." She shivered at the thought of her ten-year-old cousin. The boy lived to cause embarrassment for her. "My aunt is always swooning or inventing some new disease she's certain she has. She takes to her bed more often than not, which means the boy runs amok half the time." She shook her head. "There's been talk Uncle will take her to Bath or Brighton before the year is out to improve her health."

Beatrice snorted. "We cannot choose who we're related to." Her grin widened. "Besides, soon Mr. Geoffrey Ansley will take possession of my house. You'll be neighbors. Perhaps you and he will form a friendship." She waved a hand. "After all, you'll be twenty and seven soon. He's not that much older, perhaps five years or so. I'm not quite certain, for father refuses to talk of him."

"I highly doubt we shall be friends." Elinor yanked her hands from Beatrice's. "If he's your kin, why must you leave?"

Shadows passed over her friend's pretty face. She rolled her blue eyes. "Let's just say there is bad blood through the family. Father is merely a far-removed cousin, and even that relationship is distant and not strong enough for a claim on the inheritance. Once the old earl's will was finally read and his sons gave in with the realization this property wouldn't be going to them, the solicitors tossed it to Father until the heir could be located. Father was only a caretaker of sorts."

Elinor frowned. "Why was there such a problem with the will? Didn't the old earl like his sons enough to give them this property?"

"Oh, he adored his two sons, but this Mr. Ansley is apparently a bastard by-blow from the sons' governess at the time." Beatrice shrugged. "You can imagine the bumblebroth that resulted. I believe the governess fled to America with her boy."

Mild curiosity gripped Elinor, as her family hailed from America as well. "Why did Mr. Ansley return then? I'd think after abysmal treatment he wouldn't want to set foot in England."

"The old earl apparently had a fondness for Geoffrey regardless of how doing so for a bastard would look to Society, so he left this property to him in the will, after the fact. I guess as an apology that he couldn't acknowledge him when he was alive. You should hear what Father has to say about that." Beatrice's laugh tinkled through the parlor. Elinor's stomach clenched. She'd miss that laugh. "No matter that the earl flouted convention or the reasons he did so, this is what happened, so now my family is going to London, and I'm setting up housekeeping with William."

It seemed her friend led a charmed existence. She had plenty to look forward to. Elinor forced a swallow into her tight throat. "I'm happy for you." And she truly was. Beatrice deserved to have all her dreams come true. Still, Elinor tamped a niggle of jealousy. Why couldn't her dreams be met as well? Unable to sit still, she sprang from the settee then wandered to the window. The rain came down heavier. She crossed her arms over her chest. Why did everyone she loved vanish from her life?

"Will you be all right? You've been so sad since you lost your brother. I feared, at times, you'd do harm to yourself." Concern wove through Beatrice's voice.

Elinor turned as an image of her ginger-haired brother floated into her mind. He'd perished from a fall off a horse six months after they'd lost their parents, all of them taken too soon, but she'd always remember him as laughing and lively. "I've had much time to make peace with his—and my parents'—loss." She leaned back against the window. The cool glass felt wonderful through her clothes, and the contrast on her heated skin sent goose flesh racing along her arms. "I have no need for your worry."

"Perhaps, but I do anyway." Beatrice traced an abstract pattern on her skirt. "I'd feel better about leaving you if you would just attend local social functions and find a man you can set your heart on." She worried her bottom lip. "You need love in your life."

Elinor rolled her eyes. "I told you long ago I'll probably never marry." Why would she want to love someone to distraction only to have fate yank them from her? "I don't think I could survive another loss."

"You'll change your mind once you meet the right gentleman."

"Perhaps, but at the moment, I have no plans to discover if you're right." The thought of putting herself back on the Marriage Mart, and especially at her advanced age, chilled her heart with terror. "I'm on the shelf besides. Couple that with my allegedly unbalanced mental state and no man would want to be within a mile of me." Which was why she hadn't tried very hard to correct the gossipmongers when they'd put forth those stories. It was so much easier to let the rumors keep men at bay.

"Stuff and bother. There are all sorts of men in the world, and we both know you're not touched in the head." Beatrice waved a hand in dismissal. "Will you still work in the village bakery? If you continue to show an affinity for pastries, I'm certain old Mrs. Colfax will let you run it when her rheumy hands finally give out."

"Until something else catches my fancy, yes." A smile touched Elinor's lips. "I'm getting rather good at doing the scones every morning." It was a job she'd determined to conquer after failing miserably at her first few attempts. Mrs. Colfax had instructed her as to the correct way to make them, never failing in patience, and finally Elinor had the gist of it. "In fact, I expect my batch tomorrow morning to be perfect." She took pride in the pastry work, and for the moment, it kept the cold void inside her at bay and beat back the darkness creeping in on her soul.

That, and the secret she'd discovered from her wandering fingers.

The knowledge only she harbored widened her smile. Perhaps bringing herself to release a couple times a week was the trick of keeping her sanity, except what she felt when touching her nubbin or penetrating her core with her fingers wasn't exactly sane. That free falling moment just before she shattered must surely be considered madness, as her common sense and fears melted away with each flutter and contraction through her channel.

Never had she been so grateful from overhearing a conversation between maids. That little bit of clandestine gossip she'd come upon six months ago had been her saving grace. As of yet, pleasuring herself remained her secret, and she'd go to great lengths to keep it that way. Otherwise, it might be seen as something tawdry or depraved instead of the wonderful gift it was. The sensations that swamped her when the touch of her fingers made her fly were real. She could control those feelings, and in a reality where everything seemed beyond her control, Elinor lived for those fleeting moments. Tingles of anticipation shot down her spine to lodge between her thighs. If her uncle or aunt ever found out she was a wanton behind her closed bedroom door, they'd have her committed to a convent for insanity and to keep her out of further scandal.

Except, no one suspected. It was her naughty secret to keep, and she would as long as she had breath.

"I'm glad to hear you've found something as a hobby," Beatrice continued as if she didn't notice Elinor's reflective silence.

She stifled hysterical laughter. What would her friend say to know the nature or direction of Elinor's thoughts? Did Beatrice know the secret as well? Fear of being laughed at or preached to kept her from asking. She studied the blonde, but of course, there were no outward signs that she pleasured herself too. "Yes. So am I."

"But nothing compares to the feeling of a man's arms around you, or the sound of his voice in your ear, or him holding you while dancing," Beatrice added. She stood and shook out her skirts. "Just promise me you'll take advantage of the situation if you should happen to meet an eligible gentleman."

"Good Lord, I promise. It's not like my looks are so striking men come from far and wide simply to gaze at me with adoration."

Beatrice swatted Elinor's arm. "Oh hush. With your red hair and porcelain skin, not to mention those dreamy brown eyes, how could you not be a raging success with the men? Never mind what the gossips say. What you need is a Season in London. Perhaps you can cajole your uncle into sponsoring you."

"He's quite brow-beaten by my aunt. Even if he was willing, she wouldn't endorse such an extravagant waste. Besides, I had two Seasons when my parents were alive. I didn't take, so what would I do in London now that I'm way too old for the Marriage Mart? I rather enjoy my freedom here, such as it is. I can read or hide myself away if I'm not feeling inclined to receive visitors. I would imagine in London, I'd be under severe watch all the time."

"This is true, and the social engagements would make you surly instead of sweet. You know how you get when you're in a temper." Her friend cocked an eyebrow. "Perhaps there is a local man in the village. Does anyone come into the bakery as a habit or especially to see you?"

"Ugh, don't remind me." Elinor shuddered. "The constable's son—Michael—visits every morning without fail. Also, without fail, he states his case to me, shifting his weight, then finally asking my permission to go for a drive or a kiss or even my hand."

"That might be pleasant... if you can ignore the under bite that gives him the look of a bulldog." A giggle escaped Beatrice.

"Among other things." Elinor thought about his dirty fingernails and the constant odor of horse manure that clung to his boots. "Most definitely, he is not for me. So, every morning, I politely decline his offer, but Lord, I'm running out of excuses." Deep in her heart of hearts, she hoped she'd meet a man who'd cherish her and promise to protect her from all the bad things in the world and who was also handsome and good and smelled pleasant. If he could make her fly as she did with her own fingers, all the better. But, for whatever reason, meeting such a man hadn't happened, and no amount of wishing would make it so. Besides, she'd become rather skilled in being alone.

"Too many rejections will make Michael churlish. Mind your steps around him." Her friend frowned, a line of worry appearing between her eyebrows.

"I can soothe him if he gets into a temper."

Beatrice snorted. "Will you hit him with a broom again as you did two weeks ago? That has gone a long way into having everyone believe you're mad, you know."

"I know, but if it's necessary, I will." Elinor smiled. Michael had deserved that treatment since we wouldn't keep his hands to himself. "Besides, I've never known him to turn down a basket of day-old scones. Now, stop being such a mother hen."

"Very well, but you'll write regularly, won't you?" Beatrice bounded over to Elinor and grabbed one of her hands. "It just won't be the same without hearing your stories all the time."

"Yes, I promise to write." She linked her arm with Beatrice's. "Walk me back home. It'll be our last adventure through the tunnel." The space ran the half of a mile underground between her home and Elinor's. Most likely used long ago by smugglers or highwaymen to store their ill-gotten gains, the tunnel was overgrown with moss and mold in some places, and part of it had fallen into disrepair, but none of her family members knew of it. It had become a welcome escape when life's disappointments had come calling.

The look Beatrice sent her sparkled. "One of these days, that tunnel will get you into trouble, but not more than the secret passageway." But she accompanied Elinor out of the room, down the hall then into the library. "I told you months ago to stop using both."

"Yes, but I told you months ago that it was a vastly easier way to travel between our two houses. Plus, the passageway is fun to spy on Aunt and Uncle. Many a time I've convinced my nephew there's a ghost in the house merely because I play the part of the ghost." The passage broke off in two branches inside Beatrice's home—one on the downstairs and one upstairs. Perhaps some long ago suitor put in the passages, or perhaps the residents had been merely paranoid. It had one last outlet at the edge of the bramble that provided the border between her property and Beatrice's. Sometimes, if Elinor didn't want to breathe in the stale, musty air of the tunnel or tried to avoid the puddles and leaks when it rained, she exited there and walked the rest of the way home outside.

Elinor moved across the room to the fireplace. After unlinking arms with Beatrice, she pressed a spot in the wainscoting and took a step backward as a portion of the paneling popped out. She swiftly pulled the small door outward. "After you."

Beatrice ducked down then slipped into the darkened passage beyond. "Don't forget the candle."

"There's already one inside on that little shelf built into the stone." Elinor joined her friend in the passage. Once she closed the panel behind her, pitch black gloom swallowed her.

Late October, 1820

As quietly as she could, Elinor made her way through the secret passage. Her new neighbor had chosen today for moving into the manor house. Not having anything else to occupy her attention, Elinor traversed the passageway and now stood in the cool, cramped area on the other side of wall outside the foyer. After she'd slid the slim panel aside—which opened a screen that looked into the area—Elinor studied the few people assembled.

A man in black-and-royal blue livery appeared to be the new butler. He directed the footmen in the placement of boxes and trunks. Some were dispatched up the stairs while others where sent down various corridors. Elinor frowned. Too bad she couldn't see what the trunks contained. It was always exciting to find oneself faced with bound, mysterious trunks.

All that paled when another man entered the foyer. She'd never seen a more arresting male. A brown tailcoat stretched over his wide shoulders. An orange-and-cream striped waistcoat gave way to fawn-colored riding breeches that hugged every inch of his legs. His muscled thighs captured her attention. Was he an avid horseman? She spent more than a few seconds admiring that portion of his anatomy. She'd give anything for a glimpse of this man *sans* clothing, not that she'd seen any man naked. There simply weren't that many candidates to spy upon or that she'd want to. Sensation slid up her spine. Warmth snuck into her lower belly. When was the last time simply gazing at a man affected her? She stifled a snort. Never. Men around the village were decidedly not as appealing as this man. Then, Elinor slid her gaze slightly upward, resting it on the apex of those fantastic thighs. Though modesty demanded she stop staring at the front of his breeches, she ignored the need for proper behavior. After all, she was hidden, and what harm would it do to allow her mind to wander? Was he married? Did he possess a mistress? What did his length look like in its resting state or even when he was aroused?

Oh, good heavens! She gasped then quickly tamped any more sound before she gave away her position. She had no business wondering about him, especially not anything regarding his nether region. As heat seeped into her cheeks, she quickly focused on his face. Blond hair done in the latest style but rather unruly, as if he'd not had it cut recently, covered his head with one lock flopping over his forehead despite his efforts to brush it back. A strong jaw and aristocratic nose drew her gaze. Sensual lips had her catching her breath from fantasizing what they'd feel like on hers, but the powerful force of his green eyes held her captive. With his hands planted on his hips, he stood near the butler, surveying the immediate area with a hawk-like gaze as if he wanted furniture placement just so.

When he swept his gaze over the wall and slowly slid it past the tiny screen hiding her face, Elinor's breath stalled. Could he see her? Did he know a person spied on him from behind the wall? She trembled as she imagined him looking through the wall and finding her, raking that incredibly intense gaze over her body. She trembled. Would he find her lacking, as most of the village men did, or would he think her pretty?

Don't be silly. A man such as he wouldn't look twice at me. Especially not once the area gossips spread their poison to him regarding her family. The Bennetts were, for all intents and purposes, transplanted, newly rich Americans. Though her father had made his fortune at shipping in the New World, it hadn't been enough to buy his way into the British Peerage, regardless that many people had laughed and outright told him it wouldn't be possible anyway. Father had tried hard to ingratiate himself with high born lords and aristocrats, but they'd shunned him. He could never be part of their clubs or groups. Too bad his early demise had gotten the family further in Society than he'd ever been able to do, thanks to his wife's brother and a vacant piece of property. Not titled, but wealthy enough to be of some import to the country society who perhaps wished to further their own connections.

Elinor rolled her eyes. Still, proper gentlemen avoided her as if she'd contracted the plague regardless of how great a dowry her father had bestowed upon her. Most of the time, the disparity in positions didn't bother her. To her way of thinking, the British aristocracy was too high and a might stuffy to get on with anyway. At other times, like now, when she spied on the most beautiful man she'd seen in her life a vague ache settled in her heart. *I won't be good enough for him.* Not that she intended to introduce herself or form a relationship of any kind.

Finally, he turned away to answer a question the butler put forth. The soothing tone of his voice broke through her musings, and Elinor sagged against the wall. Good Lord he was potent. Just the sound of his voice sent goose flesh racing along her skin. She wanted to know more about him if only to feed her fantasies once she was safely tucked behind her bedroom door in the dark of night. Again, she peeked through the screen, listening intently to the conversation.

"I don't care how difficult it will be, Beasom. My study is off limits to everyone save me. I'll decorate it or not as I so chose. It's my one damn sanctuary from the rest of this torturously annoying world." A hint of an American accent clung to his clipped tones.

Oh, an American! Would that mean the newly arrived gentleman wouldn't be as unapproachable or stuffy as English men?

The butler drew himself up to his full height. He clasped his hands behind his back. "Very well, Mr. Ansley, but I must tell you that there will be certain things expected of you. You cannot just be a barrister."

The handsome man raked a hand through his hair. "Leave off with the lectures, Beasom. I'm not some green boy in need of raising and neither am I titled. There's no need to act a certain way, and there's certainly no reason for servants. This isn't a grand manor house."

"I am under orders by the old earl's will, sir. I'm to serve you."

"Then I'll tolerate you as long as I have patience, but I must warn you, I had been looking forward to being much alone. Besides, if I'm to understand the looks I've already received from some of the town locals, it's not as if my sudden unexpected place in country society will be respected in decent circles anyway."

Elinor shivered at the annoyance and authority in his voice. He might not be titled but he had the bearing of his sire. Her heartbeat accelerated. He'd only just arrived in Surrey and already the villagers had snubbed him? Well, he'd learn soon how things went, especially if he'd already met Lady Underhill.

"I cannot speak for them, Mr. Ansley. This property has sat empty for four months, and the reason you have it is steeped in scandal. The earl's family is beloved in Surrey."

"Ah, whereas I am not?"

The butler remained silent with a blank expression.

"Well, as luck would have it, I am part of his family." Bitterness flooded Mr. Ansley's voice.

"Perhaps, but you come from the wrong side of the blanket, *sir*." Slight censure rang in the butler's tone. The slight emphasis wasn't for respect. "Time is needed to soften the blow."

Hot anger raced over Elinor's skin. No matter how long she'd been on English soil, she would never grow accustomed to the sly insults and politics between servants and their alleged betters. She planted her gaze on Mr. Ansley's face. Had he picked up on the meaning? Did it bother him if he had?

"Thank you for the reminder. For a few seconds I'd forgotten my own history." His voice sounded graveled, as if he held back a proper set down, but that shift in emotion was enough to send fluttering pulses between her legs.

"Oh my," she whispered and pressed her thighs together to prolong the exquisite sensations. Beneath her shift, Elinor's nipples tightened. Would he bring such passion to the bedroom as he pleasured a woman? "Good heavens." She clamped a hand over her mouth at the second whispered exclamation.

Shut up, Elinor. You'll give yourself away.

Mr. Ansley cocked an eyebrow. He sent another glance around the room, but this time he didn't look in her direction. His lips thinned. "Somehow I suspect if I was given twenty years, public opinion of me and how I came by this property would remain the same, especially if people persist on dredging up every little detail." He stepped aside as a couple of footmen marched through the foyer with a huge trunk between them. "Please place that in my rooms. It contains my law books."

Beasom rocked forward. "Shall I place them on shelves?"

"No, thank you. I'd rather take responsibility for my own items." The blond man made ready to follow the footmen, but the butler cleared his throat and stayed him.

"Do you require all rooms aired?"

"To what purpose?" A creased marred the smooth perfection of Mr. Ansley's brow as he turned to face the other man. "I will not use them immediately."

"I assumed you wished to entertain as soon as you're settled. We've not taken the sheets from the furniture in most rooms." The butler's tone had turned rather snobbish. "Only your rooms, the parlor, the drawing room, and the dining room have been aired."

Elinor bristled. How dare the man attempt to argue with Mr. Ansley? If the handsome newcomer couldn't rub along well with Beasom, what would happen? Did he not have servants or a staff in America?

Stupid girl. It's not as if everyone in the world is wealthy enough for such things.

"That won't be necessary, Beasom. I do not intend to entertain. In fact," Mr. Ansley narrowed his eyes, "I do not wish to be disturbed while I'm in residence. No at-homes, no popping in for tea or nosy conversation. If folks around here wish to talk with me, I do require they make an appointment." He pinned the butler with an icy cold look. "You can keep my schedule, can you not?"

"I can, sir."

"Good. That will be all then."

"Thank you, Mr. Ansley."

The men exited the room and parted ways in the corridor beyond. Elinor couldn't see where either of them went.

She slid the panel back into place. What sort of man was the new resident? Would he provide enough entertainment to return to the manor and spy on him? Elinor had no idea, but the wild pounding of her heart must mean something. If nothing else, she'd come back once the household was settled and perhaps ascertain something else about the mysterious man. Not willing to leave his home just yet, she decided to spend some time exploring the remainder of the passageways in order to find out which rooms he'd selected as his sleeping chambers.

It could be useful information for future visits, and oh did she intend to visit again.

Chapter Two

Geoffrey Irvine Ansley reined in his horse as he approached a bramble hedge at the back of his newly acquired Surrey property. An hour or so earlier, all of his books, clothing, and other personal possessions had been moved into the manor, and most—with the exception of his clothes—remained in the boxes and trunks, for he hadn't had the stamina or time to put them away. The previous butler, Beasom, had kept his attention on other things. In his words, Mr. Ansley needed to learn such things 'for the proper running of the household.' An excruciatingly long two-hour tour of every nook and cranny of the manor had commenced. After yet another veiled derogatory comment about his birth, Geoffrey had dismissed the man immediately, vowing to himself he would select his own damned staff, people who knew the value of respect no matter their place in life, instead of using inherited servants. If he even required assistance beyond a housekeeper or cook.

The two maids as well as the housekeeper had fled into the bowels of the house after Geoffrey dressed down then dismissed the butler, and he didn't recall them. He'd sort out the rest of his staff later and find out if they were worth retaining. It all came down to respect. When that didn't work, the risk of losing a livelihood often did the trick. Not that his property was an estate with hundreds of acres to manage. In fact, the two-story pile had ten rooms, ivy covering one side of the exterior and a handful of acres that, so far, had been ruled by grazing sheep and a few cows of which he wasn't entirely sure belonged to him. It was a far cry from the townhouses of New York City and the distinct buzz and determined work ethic of that city, but he was here now, and he'd give Surrey his full attention. He'd gone to the stables, had a fine piece of horseflesh saddled then proceeded to tour the acreage, despite the skies darkened with swollen rain clouds.

"I need someone to tell me how things stand in the hierarchy of Surrey," he muttered to his horse. The animal, of course, did not reply, only flicked its ears. "And a tailor. These English styles are entirely too tight." As it was, the confines of his tailcoat stretched across his shoulders and prohibited free movement.

Regardless of the few bumps he'd encountered since his arrival in Surrey, for the first time in his life, he felt good about the direction his existence was taking. He may have come to the property a bit backhandedly and folks might not take him seriously or even respectfully, but here in England, the land of his birth and early childhood, he sensed a peace in his soul he'd never had before. Perhaps this change was just what he needed to usher in the next phase of his life.

After months of having his claim to the property challenged by the new Earl of Stansbury and the earl's brother—the very men he'd grown up with—Geoffrey gave into the urge to gloat. Yes, he was the bastard son of the old earl and the woman who had been Geoffrey's former governess-turned-mother, but the earl had publicly acknowledged his existence on his deathbed and bestowed house and property. The courts had backed his claim. Now he could settle into a new life away from America.

As a flash of brilliant red among the brambles and brown, dying leaves of the autumn foliage caught his attention, he narrowed his eyes. What was that? A bit of fabric, perhaps, or a fox? Urging his horse toward the area with the slightest tug to the reins and a heel into the horse's side, he sank once more into his musings.

The house he intended to recondition and decorate to his mostly American sensibilities. Of course, being back in England made him think of happier times when the ugly realities of life hadn't intruded. Perhaps he should leave the house as it was. Devil take it. Why did things need to be so difficult?

From everything he'd seen so far, Surrey was mostly bucolic, with a pub or posting inn here and there. Farms abounded, and outside of the villages that dotted the landscape and the small business contained therein, the occasional manor house was thrown in to divide the county. Besides that, there was really nothing to capture a man's fancy in the way of the fairer sex. Geoffrey snorted, and the horse's ears flicked. Not that his last romantic dalliance had ended all that well. In fact, it died quite abruptly and violently. The Italian-born opera singer he'd kept for a few months in New York had taken it badly when he protested that she played him against her husband and a wealthy shipping magnate, neither of whom she'd told him about. When he'd broke it off, she'd thrown no less than a vase of flowers, a silver tea set—the pot full of tea at the time—plus several books at him as he retreated from their rented apartment.

Female companionship wasn't his goal at the moment. Right now, he intended to open a law practice within the manor, become a trusted barrister and help people through the trials and travails they would invariably find themselves in. As the world got bigger and people's reach expanded throughout other countries, so did their legal interests and issues. Learning the differences between British and American law, and then practicing such, would keep him busy and his mind occupied enough that he wouldn't be lonely for a bedmate. And if it didn't, his tainted lineage would keep eligible and decent women from his social circle. Barring that—and if the need for a woman did grow too strong—he might sell the property as it wasn't entailed, then use the money to live in London, maybe even take a mistress, but that would mean he'd be right back in the hustle and noise of a large city.

The puzzle had no immediate answer.

As more fortunes expanded, more previously common folk looked for ways to ingratiate themselves within the ranks of the *ton* or pretend they were such. That they'd do it, he had no doubt. Would they be accepted by people who'd gained their wealth through inheritance and advantageous marriages? He couldn't begin to say. Either way, it would force Society to change, no doubt.

That brought a smile to his lips. Newly rich. Of which he was one. Wouldn't that be one big joke? Perhaps he could change the mindset of the *ton*. Such power a new outlook would have upon those dusty old relics leading Society. Along with the house and property, his late father had bestowed quite a tidy sum on him, much to the chagrin of his *brothers*.

"Not that I have any intention of spending a farthing of that coin, Titan," he confided to the horse. "I refuse to be beholden to the new earl."

He arrived at the hedgerow in time to catch another glimpse of red. And it wasn't a scrap of fabric or a wild animal. It was, in fact, a person. "You there, miss. Do you require assistance?" he called as a young woman stood fully upright from the tangle of branches. "Did you lose your way or perhaps your horse?" He glanced around the immediate area. There was no sign of a wandering animal or even another person.

"No. I didn't lose my way. I'm exactly where I intended to be." Her brown eyes, framed by red, almost golden lashes, widened even as a lock of her gloriously red hair tumbled from its knot at her nape. A few cobwebs stuck to her tresses, but that one escaped tendril played to his thoughts. Was it silky or coarse? What would it feel like sliding over his skin and would it smell of flowers? "I just didn't expect you to be here when I emerged."

"Emerged?" What an odd choice of words. "Emerged from where? Where were you before?" He frowned.

"It doesn't matter." She smoothed a hand down the front of her drab, brown dress. Dust and cobwebs clung to the fabric. A smudge of dirt streaked across one cheek. "If there won't be anything else, Mr. Ansley?" An American accent hung in her voice. How very odd to find a transplant here at the edge of his property.

Though all he could think about was wiping away that smudge, the "Mr. Ansley" yanked the thought from his mind.

Did she know him? Geoffrey wound the reins around his left hand, fighting the impatient dance of his horse. "I beg your pardon, but have we already met? It would seem you have the advantage of me." He would have remembered someone as striking as her. That red hair called to him, fascinated him. He'd never known anyone, female or male, with ginger hair. Did her temper match the fiery color? Would the curls between her thighs be as bright?

Leave off, Ansley. You're not looking for a bedmate at the moment.

"Uh..." The woman held her bottom lip between her teeth. He couldn't be certain, but he thought he caught the hint of a blush staining her cheeks, and it made her unremarkable face suddenly come into personality. "No, we have not met, but yes, I do know of you and the fact you just moved to Surrey." She gave him a nod then crossed her arms over her chest, which only drew his attention to the bodice of her dress. The swell of her breasts heated his blood. He imagined what they'd feel like against his palm and was obliged to shift in the saddle as his groin hardened. "I am Miss Elinor Bennett."

"Ah." He had no recollection of the name. "I'm Geoffrey Ansley, and you have stumbled upon my property. Do you live around here?" She hadn't told him what she was doing lurking about his hedgerow, and unattended as well. "Can I escort you home? It's the least I can do, for it looks like rain any moment." Damnable English weather, but he'd suffer it gladly for the chance to spend another few minutes in this enchanting creature's company.

"Yes, I do live near." She openly studied him with a frankness and curiosity he found refreshing and not all at unpleasant. Though he waited for her to smile, she never did, and disappointment crushed him. "I'm afraid I must return—without your assistance. Thank you for the offer." Miss Bennett scrambled the rest of the way out of the brambles until she reached the relatively clear ground of the field.

"Where?" Was she a villager or perhaps one of the farmers' daughters, one of the area gentry out for a lark? Never had he the urge to kiss a woman so strongly, and this from only a few minutes in her company when he knew nothing about her other than her name. Geoffrey tamped the hot lust rising in his body. It wouldn't do to give the gossipmongers proof that he had no manners. He wasn't a rake or a rogue, and he certainly wasn't in the immediate need for a romance, though he might change his mind if an opportunity to charm the chit presented itself.

"Just over the fields." She backed away, putting quick space between them. "Perhaps I shall see you at social functions or even in Town for the upcoming Season."

"I do not care for the idea of Seasons—Little or Big. Too much trolling for fortunes and position. It kills the excitement and the novelty of a first meeting when one knows everything down to the last farthing a family has behind them as well as their connections." He held her gaze as he spoke. Was that only polite interest lighting her brown eyes, or was it curiosity in him? "For the conceivable future, Surrey is my home and will be the source of my social engagement."

"Well, good evening then." Miss Bennett turned and pelted over the newly harvested field. Her skirts flapped about her ankles and her backside swayed.

Damnation, she was a fine piece. He shifted in the saddle.

Geoffrey followed her retreat with his gaze then flicked his attention to the gray rooftop in the distance. Did she live there? If so, was her family prominent in the area? He supposed he'd find out as a matter of course, and no amount of pondering would provide the answers. With a flick of the reins and a forceful heel into his mount's side, he wheeled the horse around and headed for home. At least she hadn't looked at him with pity or disgust in her eyes. That was something.

Later that evening, still restless, Geoffrey walked into one of the local pubs that Guildford had to offer. It seemed the busiest of the three, and the rich, meaty scent of roasting meats made the decision for him. As soon as he settled at one of the tables and had given his order for a hearty shepherd's pie and a tankard of ale, he sighed in contentment. He might enjoy some aspects of America better than England, but only the British could make a decent shepherd's pie.

He glanced around the room. Men of all classes filled the area. Food and beer were the common levelers. The buzz of conversation permeated the air. Occasionally, barks of laughter punctuated the noise. Above all, none of the patrons shot him sour looks or whispered as soon as they saw him. Perhaps these would be his contemporaries. He grinned, nodding his thanks as a barmaid brought the tankard of ale. This was what England felt like to him, what it should always be in his memories. The camaraderie and warmth reminded him of those early days with his governess—the woman who he'd discovered later was his mother. Why couldn't his brothers and old acquaintances see he was just as much victim of circumstances as anyone else? He'd asked for none of this.

After washing down the bitter taste of his later childhood with a swig of ale, Geoffrey cast another glance around the room. A man, immaculate in green tailcoat, gold waistcoat and tan trousers, separated from his table of cronies and came toward him. He swaggered, for that was the only way to describe his confident movement, as he approached Geoffrey's table then paused in front of it with an easy smile on his face. "Hello there. You have the look of a man content with life. Mind if I inquire as to why?"

"I am fairly content. You're quite correct." Geoffrey nodded. "Please sit." He waited until the brown-haired fellow settled himself in the chair opposite, then said, "I'm newly arrived in Surrey. Mr. Ansley, if you must know."

"Mr. Ansley!" A man hailed him in a jovial voice. "The local gossip mill is buzzing about you."

"I imagine they are." Geoffrey frowned. Was there no one else in all of Surrey for the gossip mongers to chew upon? "Please, call me Geoffrey. I'd rather not stand on ceremony or formality here."

"Ah, the new landowner in town. I've heard the rumors regarding your sudden inheritance." Undisguised interest coated the man's voice and his gray eyes sparkled.

"Oh?" Geoffrey's gut clenched. Would this evening turn into a debate on whether he should own the property? "I have the letter from the old earl's solicitor as well as the nod from the courts. My right to be here is quite official."

"Oh, I don't doubt it is, and you won't get a challenge from me. But, if I were you, I'd not pay the rumormongers a mind. You'll find Surrey has the most gossips per mile in all of England."

"That's what I'm afraid of. No chance of burying myself in the country and keeping everyone at bay."

"Small-minded folks reside here, but then, there are many good and kind people too. Seek them out instead." The other man extended a hand. "I'm Stephen Tarkington. From near Cranleigh, but here visiting an acquaintance of mine before leaving for London on holiday with my lady fair."

"Sounds like you're looking forward to the time away." Geoffrey shook the proffered hand, and his was pumped within a vigorous grip. No more was said as the barmaid delivered his shepherd's pie. He thanked her then inhaled the aroma of braised meat and potatoes.

"You could say that. At times, country life is more exhausting than life in Town."

"You're right on that count. Pardon me." He cast a glance to his companion. "I haven't had dinner yet today, and I'd assumed I'd be dining alone." With his thoughts pleasantly occupied by the red-haired woman he'd talked with earlier.

"Don't mind me." Stephen didn't appear ruffled. "I had the same thing for my dinner, and you won't be disappointed."

Geoffrey nodded. He tucked into the pie with gusto, and it was every bit as hearty and satisfying as he'd thought. Just like he remembered from his childhood. "So, you've had your own problems with the area rumormongers?" It was as good a place as any to start a conversation, since it didn't appear his new friend would leave any time soon.

"Oh yes." Stephen's grin widened. "I arrived in Surrey in May then promptly found myself courting a woman quite used to scandal, Lady Maggie Parker." He shrugged. "After a bit of a sticky wicket involving her niece and one of the area's most prominent gentry," he dropped his voice to a whisper, "and a run at a very erotic courtship."

Geoffrey gawked. Since when did Englishmen rush to give out such personal confidences? "Is that information you're comfortable sharing?"

Stephen chuckled. "It's widely known, and since you're new here, you may as well hear it from me." His grin widened. Apparently, the man wasn't offended or embarrassed. "I offered for the lady. We were wed this past month. And I must say, I never thought I'd enjoy being leg-shackled so much."

"I'd say it worked out well for you." Geoffrey took another bite of pie then chewed thoughtfully. "I've not been in the county long enough to hear stories of your exploits. Did you and your lady turn Surrey on its ear?"

"You could say that we did." Stephen seemed like a man in the grips of supreme contentment. His easy smile and happy expression couldn't be denied. He leaned forward, placing his forearms and hands on the tabletop. "And I have to say, it was the best gamble I ever took."

"Good to hear." Geoffrey sipped his ale. "The task of finding a woman to be by your side for a lifetime is quite daunting at times."

"It is." Stephen rapped a knuckle on the table. "Let me guess. You've yet to find your own lady. Am I correct in that thinking?"

Despite the rather intrusive subject matter, Geoffrey nodded. "I have not." He shoveled another bit of pie into his mouth, chewed then swallowed it and laid down his fork. "Months ago, I had a mistress, but the liaison did not end well."

"I'm sorry to hear that."

Geoffrey waved away the other man's concern. He wiped his mouth with a rough linen napkin. "It was for the best. She enjoyed the company of two other men in addition to mine. It may be dim of me to say, but I'd like the lady in my protection to grant me the honor of an exclusive relationship." Of course, if the woman in question never let on she was attached in the first place, it wouldn't be that exclusive. He shook his head. No use worrying about his past mistakes now.

"Well, a man does want that possessive claim." Stephen's expression sobered. "I wasn't certain I wished to marry, but after meeting Maggie, I changed my mind. There's just something about her I adore and cannot live without."

A stab of jealousy shot through Geoffrey's chest. "Marriage is a noble goal, of course, but I'm afraid no woman in her right mind would take a second look at me—if I were in the market."

Stephen narrowed his eyes. "Why? You have all your teeth and haven't developed a paunch as yet, and your hair is all your own. You're a prime catch."

"Well, thank you for that." Geoffrey snorted with laughter. It had been a while since he'd been gripped with humor so deep. "I meant with my pedigree clouded with controversy, decent women won't look twice at me, and if they do, I'm sure their friends and well-meaning family members will set them straight." He shrugged. "Perhaps my solution is to find a woman who is touched in her upper stories. At least then, it won't occur to her to question the rumors."

"Indeed." Stephen stroked a hand along his jaw. "If you're serious, there is a young woman nearby—a Miss Elinor Bennett in fact. According to the gossip mill, she's quite mad. Perhaps it's living in a house that's reputed to be haunted or because she lost her immediate family to horrible accidents within six months of each other, I don't know. But with all that red hair, one does wonder."

"Oh?" Geoffrey sat straighter. "I had the occasion to meet her briefly earlier this afternoon. And yes, she does have the most glorious hair." Even now, as the image of her popped into his head, his cock tightened.

"Did you find her batty?"

"Actually, no. I did not." Except for the stint in the hedgerow, he found her polite and pleasant. If she was mad, did it matter to him? A surge of protective instinct welled within him. Perhaps she'd merely not had the proper help she needed. "She didn't seem inclined to chat, and shortly after we introduced ourselves, she fled across the field."

Stephen chuckled. "I know that light in a fellow's eye. You have more than a passing interest in the woman."

"Perhaps. I only know she has pleasing features." He didn't want to reveal his feelings to a relative stranger.

"Well, if you are in earnest, I recommend getting to know her better, since she is your closest neighbor. From what my wife tells me, Miss Bennett lives with her uncle and aunt as well as their young son." He stood then pushed in his chair. "In the interest of being neighborly, perhaps you should pay a call on them."

Geoffrey nodded. "I was extended an invitation by a Mr. Cecil Adelaide to discuss the local area and perhaps be taken around to the prominent gentry. I assume he's a man of influence in Surrey?"

"Then all to the good. Adelaide is the chit's uncle. He's not gentry, but he does have enough coin to cause folks to listen to what he has to say. It's a tailor-made situation. Go take tea with the family." Stephen clapped Geoffrey on the shoulder. "Worth the chance. If nothing else, you can spend the time watching her from across the room and fantasizing about her later."

"Thank you, I think." Long after the other man had departed, Geoffrey stared at the empty chair he'd occupied without really seeing it.

Was Miss Bennett the answer to companionship, or was it just fanciful imagination that he remembered the flash of interest he'd spied in her eyes when they'd met? And was she truly mad like Stephen had indicated? If so, beauty and gorgeous hair wouldn't be enough to mask crazy, but he'd help her find her way in local society if he could.

The problem needed much more pondering over much more ale.

Chapter Three

Please don't notice me.

"Elinor, will you be a dear and see that Nigel is dressed properly for his French tutor? Monsieur Deparee will arrive within the hour, and I just haven't the strength to entertain today."

Elinor cringed in the hallway outside her aunt's bedchamber. She'd thought to sneak past on her way downstairs, but one of the floorboards had creaked and gave away her position. She bowed her head. "Actually, Aunt Fran, I'm overdue for the bakery this morning." Appalled at how easily the lie tripped off her tongue, she poked her head into her aunt's bedroom. The slim woman lay propped against a mound of pillows, her dark hair perfectly arranged, looking for all the world as hale and hearty as if she'd just come in from a horseback ride. *Declining in health my arse.* It seemed her aunt was merely lazy.

A frown pulled at the corners of her aunt's mouth. "I was under the impression you had this morning free. Not that I condone joining the working class. You don't need to lower yourself like that."

Think, Elinor. She chewed her bottom lip. "I did, but you how old Mrs. Colfax is. She completely forgot she was to visit her sister so I told her I'd fill in. And it's not lowering myself. I do enjoy getting out of the house and doing something besides finding new ways to muck up my embroidery work. Waiting around for something to happen just isn't for me." She waved to her aunt. "I should return in a few hours. Not later than noon I should think." *I'll hide in the passageway until then.*

Never had she torn down the stairs so quickly. Only once did her heel snag in her skirt, and she slipped off one step, but after grabbing the railing, she righted herself then continued on her way. At the ground floor, she cast a glance about the area then slunk into the parlor. At this time of morning, her uncle would already be out of the house. He usually rode horses with Baron Underhill each morning to discuss politics and whatever else men talked of. She pulled a face as she thought of the name. Her dear uncle had the dim-witted idea that she might enjoy being matched with one of the baron's strapping, but slow, sons. To date, the baroness had staunchly refused such a thing. Most likely it was because the thought of marrying off one of her sons to "American rubbish" turned her stomach. A snicker escaped. There was much more that made a person trash than their roots.

And Elinor couldn't agree with the unsuitable nature of a match more. Those two young men might possess brawn and *sans* clothing would undoubtedly make a girl's heart race, but without a brain between the two, she wanted nothing to do with them. They couldn't compare to the newly arrived Mr. Ansley. Not only did he have a body worthy of a swoon, but she suspected he was smart as well. Hadn't Beatrice mentioned he was a solicitor or such in America?

Merely thinking of him sent shivers dancing over her skin. She drew her gray wool shawl tighter around her shoulders as she slipped over the parlor floor to the panel near the fireplace. With another quick glance over her shoulder, she touched the hidden mechanism, and the panel popped open. Elinor ducked inside the passageway then pulled the panel closed behind her.

Thick, musty-scented darkness enfolded her along with a pronounced chill in the gloomy air. With shaking hands, she felt for the ledge. When the familiar shape of a matchbox met her fingers, she grabbed it, took out a match then struck one, and after the light flared, she lit an oil lantern, blew out the candle then fit the glass over the wick of the lamp. The pitch-black passageway loomed before her, but at the other end was Mr. Ansley's property, and if she was lucky, she'd get a glimpse of him as well.

Two days had passed since she'd met him at the edges of their land, and in those two days, she'd thought about no one else except him. As she walked along the cold passageway, Elinor pondered the implications of the problem. She'd discovered which bedroom he'd claimed as his and about what time he left the house each morning. Yesterday, around noon, she'd spied on him while he'd written letters in his study. He'd left the dust sheets in place over bookcases and chairs, only uncovering the desk and the massive leather-bound chair behind it.

She didn't remember how long she'd simply stood at the screen behind his desk, watching. Not once did he break his concentration. She imagined herself brushing back the wayward lock of hair that kept falling over his brow or working the stiffness from his shoulders he undoubtedly had from hunching over the desk. He never seemed to feel her gaze, but she'd kept him company all the way through him folding his correspondence, slipping it into envelopes then sealing them with wax. When he'd lifted his arms over his head and stretched, and his tailcoat pulled taut over his shoulders, she'd caught her breath, feasting her gaze on the play of his muscles. Oh, he was easy on the eyes. Once sufficiently relaxed, he'd stacked his letters in a tidy bundle. Afterward, he'd left the study and hadn't returned. Elinor had had no choice except to go back to her house.

The minutes through the passage passed quickly, mostly since her new neighbor occupied her mind. Was he attached? Did he enjoy his return to England? What would he think of her and her secret should she ever reveal it? Not long afterward, she arrived at Mr. Ansley's manor. Since it was not yet nine-thirty and, if the last two days were any indication, he would have already returned from his morning ride, she quietly snuck up the narrow stone stairs that led to the second floor of the house. If she was lucky, she could catch him as he washed his face and upper body in the basin. Yesterday, she'd been too late and had arrived just as he'd donned his shirt, depriving her of seeing his torso in all its naked glory.

Silently, she arrived at the wall of his bedroom. Not only was there a screen for spying on this room, but there was also a panel that opened into it. She'd not gone as far as to invade the room, even when he'd not been in attendance, but she'd certainly thought of it. Now, Elinor set the lantern on the roughly hewn stone floor, cringing as it made a faint clunk. Then, she stood upright, slid the slim rectangular panel aside and peered through the lattice-work screen. She sucked in a surprised breath and nearly gave herself away. If she hadn't stifled the squeak, she would have.

Mr. Ansley was in a state of undress, but even more startling, he was completely nude and reclining in a claw-footed bathtub, his knees above the water line, the long side of the tub running parallel with the fireplace and therefore her hiding spot. Yes, it was scandalous seeing the man in such a private moment, but the fact that he wasn't doing much soaping of his gorgeous body was even more so. Oh no. He was slowly stroking his member—his very stiff, very erect, very aroused member, which only grew even more so with each pass of his hand.

Elinor drew back, briefly closing her eyes. *Oh dear heavens! What should I do?*

She swallowed, but no amount of moisture could assuage her dry throat. Common courtesy demanded she return to her house and leave this man in piece, yet her curiosity was as rampant as his cock. It made her feel wicked to think about such a naughty word. Stifling a giggle at thinking the coarse term for his penis she'd learned from the maids, Elinor dared to look through the screen again. What did that hard length feel like? Would it fill her palm? What would happen if she touched it? Was it warmer than the rest of him? A furious blush fired her cheeks. Not that she would have the opportunity to touch any part of him. Never in her wildest imaginings did she think she would ever spy on such a thing as this. What would her aunt say if she found out that not only was Elinor prying into a private moment of a neighbor?

She moved her gaze back to the bathtub.

Mr. Ansley continued to stroke his hand along his shaft. Every so often, he'd tug on his cock then he'd dip his hand below the water line to squeeze his balls. His eyes were slitted, his jaw slack as he returned to his length and pumped with greater urgency. With each movement, water splashed. With every pass of his hand over the pale flesh, awareness swept along Elinor's skin. Her entire concentration remained on his hand, stroking up and down his cock, or on his thumb as he massaged the wide head.

That part of him is as beautiful as the rest of him.

Heat swept over her body the longer she gawked. Her breath shallowed, and she made a concentrated effort to remember not to make a sound. Biting her lip to reinforce the reminder, she slipped a hand beneath her shawl and slid it under the neckline of her dress. She glided her fingers over a nipple, rubbing it until it tightened and beaded. Tingles jumped from her breasts to between her legs. Her gaze went blurry and unfocused. She pressed her free hand to her mound, but the bulk of clothing gave her no relief. Knowing that she touched her body at the same time Mr. Ansley pleasured himself gave wings to the madness building within.

As a moan emanated from his room, she snapped her attention back to him. He moved his hand faster and faster along his cock and the slap of wet skin echoed in the room. She rubbed her fingers in time across her nipple, wishing it was his mouth on her body and his hand between her legs. At least, when the maids talked about such things, they whispered how wonderful such actions were. The layers of skirting kept her from gaining access to her button, so with quick, aggravated movements she bunched the fabric until she could slip her right hand between her legs without encumbrances.

She stifled a sigh as her nubbin swelled with the merest brush of her fingers. Then she slid her hand lower to her opening. Wetness eased the movement, and she returned her left hand beneath her bodice to torment the hard nipple. A shudder raced down her spine, not only from the pleasure she brought to her own body, but also from watching Mr. Ansley as he did the same. Elinor matched his strokes. Each time he pumped his length, she plunged two fingers into her drenched passage. With her thumb, she kept pressure on her button. Her heartbeat accelerated, and she drew in a ragged breath that echoed in the closed space. In her mind it was Mr. Ansley's lips on her slick folds, his tongue teasing her swollen nub, just like she's heard the maids tell of the act, and his fingers moving in and out of her.

Fire raced through her blood, and she fluttered her fingers deep in her channel. Hot feeling swept through her body. She trained her gaze to the man in the room. His head was thrown back. A long, deep groan left his throat, and with one last jerk on his shaft, spurts of milky white liquid shot from the tip and over the edge of the tub. Elinor pinched her nipple as well as her button at the same time, imagining how his cock would feel buried deep inside her body and wondering if his seed would be warm or sticky. Tickles moved through her core, but she didn't spend. A curious feeling of restlessness remained. She didn't mind, as the sight of Mr. Ansley reclining against the back of the tub made her forget her own need.

His arms lay along the sides, his knees out of the water, and his eyes closed. His chest, with its mat of blond hair clinging to his upper torso, moved with his deep breathing. He embodied the perfect picture of a man who has just tumbled into release and was quite content at enjoying the relaxing aftermath.

And he was magnificent. She wished she were at his side, combing her fingers through the hair on his chest or pressing her lips against his temple. What would he smell like? Or even more naughty, what would he do if she climbed into the tub and straddled him, just as naked as he? Would he touch her breasts, take her nipples into his mouth? With one last brush of her wet fingers over her button, she withdrew her hand then wiped it on her petticoat.

With a moan of disappointment that her fantasies weren't real, Elinor snapped the viewing panel closed then slumped against the wall. She wrapped her shawl tighter about her body, but the residual shivers racing along her skin had nothing to do with the chill. How often did he touch himself, and would he do it tomorrow if she came at the same time? Seeing him this morning wasn't enough. The craving to continue watching him burned through her body.

Lord help me, but I'm going to be very, very naughty in the days to come. At least it would fill the aching void in her chest where her heart should be.

"Miss Bennett, one of your neighbors is here," her uncle's butler, Hoskins, said as he met her in the downstairs hall. "I've settled him in the parlor, but Mr. Adelaide is still on his walk with his wife."

Elinor rolled her eyes. "Right, the midday walk, so she can breathe in the fresh air that will hopefully restore her to perfect health." No doubt after doing this a few times, her aunt would have a miraculous recovery enough to cajole her uncle into taking her to London or Brighton or Bath for a celebratory holiday.

When she realized Hoskins still stood with an expression of polite inquiry on his face, she sighed. "What do any of these events have to do with me?"

"Perhaps you should entertain Mr. Ansley in their stead while I fetch tea."

Oh, dear heavens, our guest is Mr. Ansley?

"I... I'm not certain I can do that." She pressed a hand to her stomach as that organ threatened to send up the light lunch she'd eaten not long ago after coming out of the secret passageway. "I'm not dressed for entertaining. I have no idea what to talk about to him." Despite her nerves, a tingle of excitement tripped down her spine. He was here, in her home, the man she'd spied upon just this morning, the man with whom she'd pleasured herself while watching him do the same.

The butler, who wore his black hair slicked down with pomade and parted severally down the middle, smiled. "Every woman suffers nerves the first time she entertains, but if I may offer a suggestion?"

"Yes." Elinor nodded. She rather liked the butler, as he never judged or censured her.

"Be yourself, miss. If you affect airs, your guests will know. Talk about subjects that interest them. Before you know it, the visit will have concluded, and you won't know how the time passed so quickly."

His simple words warmed her heart. "Thank you, Hoskins." She smoothed her hands down her day dress of daffodil yellow. "I hope I'm as brilliant and witty as you believe I can be."

He nodded. "I shall bring in tea presently." The butler took a step past her then paused. "Also, Master Nigel is with Mr. Ansley. He refused to leave when I suggested other pursuits."

"Of course he did." Why, oh why, did her dratted cousin need to be present? With no other recourse, Elinor took a deep breath, squared her shoulders then proceeded down the hall. *I can do this. He doesn't know that I've spied on him or did anything else. It's just a simple social call.* Yet hoping didn't negate the nerves that fluttered her stomach. Once at the door, she paused. Her hands shook and she clasped them in front of her before entering the room. "Mr. Ansley. What a pleasant surprise." Where had the confidence in her voice come from?

"The surprise is all mine." Recognition rounded his eyes for a moment before his smile banished it. "I never thought the girl I met in the field would be my neighbor."

Heat rushed through her. "I suppose I should have told you..." Oh, those green eyes of his seemed to connect through to her soul. Her stomach quivered, but before she could add to the conversation, her cousin interrupted.

"And look at you, pretending to be the grand lady of the manor," Nigel cut in before Mr. Ansley could even stand. "Putting on airs while me mum and dad are out?"

Good Lord, what an obnoxious child. She glanced at Mr. Ansley, and after catching his bemused expression, she turned to her pudgy cousin. He had a streak of pudding on his chin and a matching stain on the front of his shirt. "Nigel, thank you for revealing the situation to our guest. Yes, until your parents return from their walk, I'm the only one available to entertain."

"Well then, introduce me." Nigel puffed out his chest and belly. His double chin grew more pronounced with his toothy grin. "After all, I'll inherit this pile of bricks one day."

She resisted the urge to roll her eyes. "Right." But when she gave Mr. Ansley her full attention, the amused twinkle in his green eyes triggered an avalanche of sensation down her spine. "I... uh." Elinor swallowed, hoping for something witty to say, but no words fell into her brain. "Mr. Ansley, this is my cousin Mr. Nigel Adelaide. Nigel, this is our new neighbor, Mr. Geoffrey Ansley. He's moved into Beatrice's home."

"I'm not an idiot, Ellie. I know where he lives." Nigel plopped down in his chair and stared at their guest with his piggy eyes.

At times, she wished her aunt and uncle had made a better effort to instill manners into their son. He'd be insufferable when he was grown. She glanced at Mr. Ansley. "I apologize for my cousin. He has the tendency to be a prick at times." When she realized she'd used less than proper language for a social call, she clapped a hand over her mouth. *My uncle will lecture me for certain.*

Mr. Ansley's deep, rich laughter flowed over her and heated her skin, and calmed her enough that she didn't respond to Nigel sticking out his tongue at her. "I appreciate the humor, especially after the welcomes I've been getting since I've arrived in Surrey." He gestured at the settee opposite the one he'd occupied. "Please, sit. I'd like to talk until your uncle arrives."

She sank on the settee near his, and was grateful for the chance since her knees were like oatmeal. "Is there a particular reason you came to call, Mr. Ansley?"

"Mr. Adelaide promised to show me around the area and to introduce me to the notables. He also advised me to throw some sort of an at-home or rout as a way of welcoming myself to the neighborhood."

"Well, my uncle does say there's no quicker way to find fast friends than over a pint or a snifter of prime brandy."

"Excellent." He resumed his seat but kept his attention on her. "I wanted to go ahead and meet everyone so that I can settle into some sort of routine."

"I see." What did two people talk about when they didn't know each other, especially when one of those people has seen the other stark naked and in an intimate moment? Her cheeks heated. She couldn't shove the image of his hand on his aroused member from her mind. "Before she left, my friend Beatrice hinted that you're a solicitor or some sort of barrister."

"Yes. In New York City, I was an attorney." He leaned forward and dangled his hands between his knees, which focused her attention to his thighs and higher still. "I hope to practice law here in Surrey, but know it will require intense study, not to mention passing the requisite exams. Helping people with legal problems is my passion. If I can assist them, then it can lessen their worry."

"What a lovely way of looking at life." The longer she stared at him, the more her cheeks blazed. Would he notice her high color, and if he did, what would he contribute it to? Despite her reaction, she smiled, for the knowledge that she'd spied on him and seen his naked body remained her secret. He didn't know that she'd seen what he looked like beneath his buff-colored trousers, the embroidered ivory waistcoat and the superfine emerald tailcoat that brought out his eyes and distracted her. At the last second, she stifled a sigh of pure bliss. Uncertain of how to proceed, she dropped her gaze to the toes of his boots.

"Lord, please don't tell me you're flirting with the man, Ellie," Nigel cut in with an infusion of shock in his customary whining tone. "Or worse yet, that you're addlepated by him."

"What?" She looked at her horrible cousin. "I'm not." And why would that make her addlepated? He was a handsome man. Any woman would find him thus.

"Liar." Nigel licked at a spot on his hand. "Your cheeks are red. Mother says when a girl's cheeks are red in the company of a gentleman, she's thinking of him improperly or trying to flirt."

A soft chuckle came from Mr. Ansley. "Insolent young man, aren't you?"

Elinor wished the floor would open and swallow her whole. Was there ever a nastier boy than her cousin? "You are quite a bother, Nigel. Don't you have chickens or kittens to terrorize?"

He snorted. "Ignore Ellie, Mr. Ansley. All the other men do."

"Why is that?" Mr. Ansley's question held mild inquiry and a touch of censure. Elinor hoped that meant he thought the boy loathsome too. He briefly glanced at her. "She's quite pleasing to the eye, don't you think?"

He thinks I'm pleasing? She couldn't help the grin pulling at the corners of her mouth.

"What? Me? No!" Nigel stuck out his tongue again. "She's hideous with all that red hair." He shook his head. "Plus, she cannot catch a man because she's queer. Runs off all her suitors if anyone's brave enough to come, not that she's had any recently. Not even her dowry can attract a man."

Oh, please stop talking you little brat! Was there anything more insufferable than a spoiled ten-year-old boy? Elinor refused to look at either Nigel or Mr. Ansley. All her earlier confidence fled and left her stomach shaking and her chin quivering. She took a shuddering breath and willed herself not to cry.

"That wasn't very polite to say in mixed company, or at all," Mr. Ansley warned.

"If it's true, it doesn't matter. I can say what I like." He puffed out his chest and the stain on his shirt grew. "It's my house, I might remind you."

"Why do you think your cousin is queer?" Mr. Ansley asked, deftly ignoring the pompous statement as if he'd not heard it.

She shot a glance at him, but no trace of anything malicious shadowed his features, merely curiosity and the same twinkling amusement in his eyes. "I'm not."

Nigel wriggled off the chair as soon as the butler entered with the tea service. "She's batty in her upper story. Clean mad most times. Doesn't go anywhere except here and the bakery in the village. Eats her mistakes, I'm told. Getting fat, she is. Just look at her." He gave Elinor a nasty look while stealing a handful of seed cakes from the tray before Hoskins could set the tray onto the table near her settee. "Not to mention, her bedroom is haunted, but she stays there anyway. Probably commands the nether world too. Who would want her?"

Elinor narrowed her eyes. "Does your mother know what a horrible boy you are?"

He stuck out his tongue, which was coated with half-chewed seed cakes.

Once the butler left the room, Mr. Ansley cleared his throat. "The world is a strange and beautiful place, Nigel." He accepted the cup of tea Elinor gave him. "Most of the time, everyone is deserving of a match and even love. Never forget that one man's bizarre is another man's marvel."

Elinor's heart skipped a beat. Did he truly mean that?

"If you think that, you're as batty as she is." Nigel returned to his chair with his pile of cakes.

"Enough, Nigel. That was impolite." Elinor frowned at her cousin. "Do you want tea?"

"Of course I do. Five sugar lumps."

She huffed. "It's a wonder your teeth haven't rotted out by now." She prepared the drink then plunked it in front of him on the table. Elinor glanced at their guest, and the soft smile tugging at his lips sent another round of flutters through her belly. "I apologize for my cousin's behavior. He fancies himself lord of the manor at times."

"Think nothing of it. This is a far cry from most of the receptions I've had since arriving." He sipped his tea and his eyes gleamed. "But perhaps this conversation is boring for someone of Nigel's superior intellect."

She didn't know what he meant by that, but if he was trying to boot the boy from the room, she would enthusiastically embrace the notion. "Perhaps you're correct, Mr. Ansley."

Elinor grinned at her cousin. "Nigel, if you wish to excuse yourself, you may."

Then she'd be alone with the man who had the power to weaken her knees, and he didn't have a clue that he did. On the other hand, perhaps asking Nigel to leave hadn't been such a good idea, for then she'd be alone with Mr. Ansley and her thoughts.

What a coil.

Chapter Four

Geoffrey schooled his shock beneath what he hoped was an expression of placid boredom. He couldn't believe how obnoxious Miss Bennett's cousin was, and how he treated her with less respect than he'd show a pig in slop. "Nigel, I'm quite certain you'd rather be in twelve other places than here, taking tea with adults while they talk of banal things like the weather or the strength of Lady Underhill's stays."

He sent a glance to Miss Bennett, pleased when she caught her lush lower lip between her teeth. Would she have laughed if not for that? He had no idea, but the thought of hearing her do so made him want to try harder. From everything Nigel had said, coupled with what he'd learned in the pub, the urge to delve into her life grew strong.

Nigel regarded him with crumbs clinging to his pudgy cheeks. "Will you talk about me when I'm gone?"

"Absolutely not," Geoffrey promised, and it was one he intended to keep. He wasn't the slightest bit interested in the little weasel. "Most likely I'll speak of appointments and dull legal affairs, or folks around Surrey and where to procure eggs."

"Very well." The boy gathered his hoarded cakes then hopped from the chair. "But the moment Mother and Father return, I'm telling them Elinor was rude to me." With a parting glance at Miss Bennett that simmered with boyish ire, Nigel quit the room.

"I owe you my thanks, Mr. Ansley." Miss Bennett took a sip of her tea then gave him a tentative grin. "Anyone who can make Nigel disappear holds wonderful power."

"Then I consider myself grateful to play the vanquishing hero against your maiden in distress." *Devil take it, where did that farcical piece of nonsense come from?* He cleared his throat. "But there is one statement I want to be certain you hear."

"Oh?" Her hand shook. She set her teacup onto its saucer and avoided his gaze.

Was she playing coy or was she truly inexperienced when it came to conversing with people not of her immediate family, especially gentlemen? Another mystery he wanted to solve. "Yes. Your cousin was most heartily wrong when he said you were fat." Geoffrey slid his gaze over her body, caressed the swell of her breasts, landed on the curve of her hip before returning to her face. Too bad she had her hands clasped in her lap and was seated, preventing him from doing a full assessment. "I think you have a pleasant figure." As before when he'd met her in the field, the urge to take her into his arms made itself known. What would those delectable curves feel like held flush against him?

"Thank you." She raised her gaze. Pleasure and shock warred for dominance in her rich brown eyes. "No one has ever said such nice things to me before."

His chest tightened at the knowledge. "They should, and often." He put his teacup onto the table. "Since we have a few minutes of time, why don't we talk about you?"

"Why?" Miss Bennett's brow furrowed. "Nigel has told you everything there is to know."

Ah, then why did color suddenly blaze into her cheeks? "Why don't you let me be the judge of that?" He scooted to the end of the settee he occupied in an effort to be closer to hers. "Why are you here playing hostess for your uncle?"

"Who else would I play hostess for?" A flash of pain flickered through her expression. The light died from her eyes. "Ten years ago, my parents died in a carriage accident." She stared at her lap while pleating her skirt in one hand. They were going up to London for a short holiday. Since Father had made his fortune in America, he found it trying to be a man of leisure in England. His ultimate dream was to catch the attention and respect of the Peers. He'd always promised Mother a splurge in London, just the two of them as a reward for uprooting our family, as people of consequence, without a Season for me attached, and finally put actions to words."

"My condolences. The roads between Surrey and London are horrid, and carriages are unstable at the best of times."

She swept her gaze upward until it collided with his. "Thank you." Her chin quivered. "They'd barely traveled out of Surrey before the accident happened. It had rained heavily the night before, and the puddles hid a deep hole in the road." She swept the tip of her tongue along her bottom lip, and Geoffrey stifled a groan. Given the topic at hand, allowing his desire to show would be ill-advised. "The wheel broke, the carriage overturned, and when the horses spooked, they dragged the equipage a quarter of a mile before the driver could run after and calm them." A tiny tremor in her voice followed the statement.

"Please, don't talk about it if it causes you such pain." He'd seen the signs: her pale skin, the worrying of her skirt, but remarkably, there was no trace of tears in her eyes. Perhaps she'd already made peace with it. After all, it was a decade ago.

"No, it's all right." She sighed. "From what the driver said later, when the carriage overturned, my mother broke her neck. She died instantly, but as my father tried to climb out and the horses ran, the carriage twisted again with the next bump on the road. He perished then."

"You are an only child?"

"Now I am." She grabbed her teacup, took a gulp then replaced it on the saucer. "My brother died six months after the carriage accident. He'd gotten into the habit of racing his fellows on horseback. He took a jump he shouldn't have and didn't clear a low-hanging branch on the other side of a creek." She shrugged. "He died of a bashed in skull."

"I'm so sorry. Such a massive amount of tragedy for one so young. What were you, seventeen?"

"Yes. Seven and twenty doesn't seem much different at times."

"Oh, but I'm sure you've had experiences that have enriched your life." Geoffrey resettled himself on the settee next to her then took up one of her hands, holding it between both of his. They both had not worn gloves. He'd removed his upon arrival. The slight dryness and redness of her palm intrigued him. Was it due to the fact she must wash her hands often at the bakery? Would she appreciate the gift of expensive lotions to soften her skin?

Get a hold of yourself, Ansley. She's not yours.

When she sent him a look of askance, he grinned. "It seemed you could use a sympathetic ear." *Dear God.* The scents of vanilla and baked goods and sugar—everything wonderful in the world—wafted from her skin. Already he was skirting the bounds of propriety sitting this close to her and actually touching her without a chaperone in the room, but he couldn't deny the urge to hold her hand. Yes, he wanted to comfort her, but now, he desired so much more.

A glimmer of a smile tugged at her mouth. "You could have given that to me from your previous position. This," she squeezed his hand, "is something more intimate." The same high color that had greeted him when she'd first entered the room blazed on her cheeks now.

"True, but there is something about a human touch that conveys what words cannot." He squeezed her hand in return, and the warmth of her skin seeped into his

"Perhaps." Miss Bennett kept her gaze on his face long enough for him to pick out tiny flecks of gold in the dark depths of her eyes.

"You miss them very much, don't you?"

"Yes, I suppose I do, when I allow myself to think of them." The muscles in her throat contracted with a heavy swallow. "I don't do that much, and try to keep so busy that when I fall into bed at night, I go right to sleep."

The need to protect her broke over him. He wanted nothing more in that moment than to wrap her in a hug and tell her life was still good and worth looking forward to or enjoying. But instead, he pushed the urge aside, uncertain of his reception. After all, he hardly knew her. "Ah, well there is something to be said about the sleep of the just and the innocent."

Her blush deepened. "Once my family was gone, my uncle—my father's brother—decided he'd take me in. We'd all come from America, you see, my father having dreams of entering the British aristocracy." Bitterness infused her chuckle. "He died without realizing that dream, but Uncle married into it, albeit somewhat removed. In a way, I suppose Father got his wish." A sigh escaped her. "Besides, Nigel had just been born by the time we arrived, and I took care of him when my aunt didn't feel like it, thereby saving them the expense of a governess later." She shrugged. "But since his wife's family has always lived in this property in some capacity, here I am."

How curious her reactions were. What was she not telling him? "Why do you work in a bakery?"

"I enjoy it there. Pastries are comforting, and except for the elderly woman who runs the place, I keep very much to myself." She pulled her hand from his. "Besides, it helps in keeping with the image that I'm mad. No one bothers me and I like it that way."

"I understand that. I'm hoping my life in Surrey will remain quiet. I'm not accustomed to the rigors of social niceties and neither do I want to encourage visitors. I require only my books to be happy."

"You don't wish to entice a wife then?" Interest crept into her voice. "I thought every man wanted to set up nurseries in order to perpetuate the line."

A blast of acrimonious laughter escaped his throat before he could recall it. "I came into this property by an inheritance after the fact, for the reason that my father wished to have a clear conscience on his death bed." Unable to sit still any longer, Geoffrey stood and fell into pacing. "Regardless, no, starting a family is not an immediate concern for me."

"You might think differently if you fall for a local lady. After all, you're a handsome man. I suspect you won't avoid the parson's mousetrap for long."

He turned and caught her gaze on him, or more specifically, on the portion of his anatomy directly below his waist before she dropped her scrutiny to the tea service. Hot lust shot through his veins, and his groin tightened with the first stirrings of arousal. "I have no interest in courtship, not that any self-respecting woman will ignore the circumstances of my birth and see the man I am." Damn it. He hadn't wanted to reveal so much about himself, but he'd gotten sucked into her soulful eyes and nearly lost his control at the sight of her lips.

Although, some exceptions could be made—not that he was intent with matrimony to the sweet Miss Bennett. Even she couldn't mask the gall that returning to England brought him due to the circumstances that had brought him back, but he would taste her tempting lips before the week was through.

A rustling at the door brought his thoughts and focus across the room. An older couple stood in the doorway. "Mr. Adelaide?"

"Indeed, my boy, and you must be Mr. Ansley. At least I hope you are; otherwise, Hoskins has told quite a hummer." The man came further into the room with a hand extended. "Glad you came calling. We have much to talk about."

Movement out of the corner of his eye stole his attention from Adelaide. Miss Bennett stood, exchanged a few soft-spoken words with the woman then left the room. He stifled a sigh. Obviously, he wouldn't be stealing that kiss today, so the question of whether her lips were as plush and soft as they looked wouldn't be answered soon.

The next morning, bored and out of sorts from his situation, Geoffrey found an ancient walking stick in the entryway then took it and walked into the village. Perhaps while he was there, he'd find a man in need of a position, as he had to fill the empty butler post. Before he could properly decide where he wanted to start his tour, the scents of sugar, cinnamon, and sweet baked goods wafted through the air and arrested his attention.

He glanced up and down the street while people bustled past. Didn't Miss Bennett work at the bakery? His heartbeat accelerated even as his stomach growled. Perhaps he should avail himself of breakfast, and in the process, grab the chance to converse with his pretty neighbor. Feeling considerably cheered, he tapped the end of the walking stick on the hard-packed street, crossed the thoroughfare then walked the short distance to the bakery.

As soon as he pushed open the scarred wooden door and entered the shop, the sweet, sensory overload swamped him. His mouth watered as he swept his gaze over the wooden counter. Some sort of muffins rested in a willow basket. A three-tiered tray filled with seed cakes occupied one corner while date scones lay cooling on wire trays nearby. Sticky buns, dripping with caramel and nuts, were lined up on a tray, clearly just out of the oven.

"Good God, where does one start when presented with such bounty?" He wasn't aware he'd spoken the thought out loud until a couple of people in line ahead of him tittered and laughed.

A short, plump elderly woman took payment for the baked goods at the opposite end of the counter from where Elinor worked. She'd just bustled in from a back room with a plate of scones. Those sparkled with a dusting of sugar, but the pastries couldn't hold his interest, not while her red hair gleamed in the sunlight streaming in through the front windows and there was a smudge of flour decorating one cheek.

She was the most beautiful woman he'd ever seen. His heart skipped a beat, and he only moved forward in the line when the patron behind him nudged his back with a growl. How bacon-brained he'd become. It wasn't as if this was the first time he'd been in her company.

By the time his turn to order came, he stood stock still as if his feet had been rooted to the ground. "Good morning, Miss Bennett."

A half smile tugged at one corner of her mouth while a pretty blush stained her pale cheeks. "Hello, Mr. Ansley." She wiped her hands on the pinafore apron that covered her torso. "What can I do for you this morning?"

Besides letting me kiss your tempting lips? He shook his head. "Which of these delights did you make?"

She glanced down the counter. Her eyes sparkled. "The sticky buns and the scones. I'm rather proud of the scones. There are date ones and cream."

"Then I shall have two of each." He planted the tip of the walking stick between his boots and piled his hands on the carved head. "How are you today?"

"Very well." She caught her bottom lip between her teeth as she put the requested scones into a box then bound it with a thick length of string. "Did you pass a good night?"

"I did. I hope you had pleasant dreams." He accepted the box from her, and when his fingers brushed hers, awareness crawled up his arm.

Her blush deepened. "Yes, very."

The man behind him cleared his throat. Then when Geoffrey didn't move away, he pushed his way to the counter. "Elinor, why do you waste time talking with this poor excuse when you will hardly give me attention?"

Geoffrey took a few steps sideways as he regarded the rude individual. Hulking and thick, the man possessed an under bite that put Geoffrey in mind of a rather ugly bulldog. "I apologize, my good fellow. Was I not conducting my affairs fast enough for you?"

The big man turned and gave him a glare. "Leave my woman alone."

His chest tightened. She belonged to this unfortunate man? "Elinor, are you spoken for by him?" He'd bring his walking stick down on the man's head if he needed to.

She rolled her eyes as she filled a box with baked goods. "Absolutely not. Michael comes in every blessed day. It's always the same thing: half a dozen scones then he either asks me for a kiss or to marry him." She shook her head and planted her hands on her hips. "I tell him the same thing—"

"No. It's always no, but I'll keep on asking because you'll change your mind sooner or later," Michael interrupted. He took the bakery box she handed him. "You can't do better'n me. My father's the Guildford constable."

"How can I forget? You tell me every bloody morning." Elinor shooed him off with a wave of her hand. "Be that as it may, I think I'll take my chances and say no again."

"You'll be sorry one of these days, Elinor. Some other girl will claim me, and you'll wish you'd accepted me."

"Perhaps. Now, go home, Michael." She slid her glance to Geoffrey. "Sorry about that. Nothing I do or say discourages him."

"Shall I defend your honor?" He grinned. Something about being in her presence calmed him and put him in a brighter mood.

"That's not necessary, but I thank you just the same. He's harmless." Her smile heated his insides. "Have a good day, Mr. Ansley." Then she glanced beyond him and gestured for the next customer.

"You too, Miss Bennett." He brought the box to his nose and sniffed. The scents of sugar and vanilla teased his nostrils. Though he hated to leave the bakery and her, the thought of consuming the scones she'd made occupied his mind. He'd have to think of another way to converse with her for a longer time.

Two days later, and under protest, Geoffrey stood at one side of a drawing room at Squire Collins' home. He'd arrived late, as he hadn't been fully certain he'd make it at all. It was a rout celebrating the squire's son's engagement. The young man, David, had apparently come up to scratch with Lady Parker-Tarkington's niece, Amanda. Geoffrey had only consented to attend because Mr. Adelaide mentioned him and his wife, plus Elinor, would be in attendance.

The opportunity to see Miss Bennett couldn't be ignored, but as of yet, he hadn't been able to talk with her. Despite trying to catch her on the public roads as she walked home from the village, his hunt had been unsuccessful. When he'd called on her uncle the day before, she hadn't been anywhere around. If the wind were personified, it would be Miss Elinor Bennett. Now, a few of the local young men hovered around her, always engaging her in conversation or a few country dances. Though she was polite, her smiles never reached her eyes. Geoffrey's heart lurched. What would it take for her to come alive?

Perhaps the bigger question was why did he want to see her do such a thing?

When she edged away from a cluster of young bucks and headed toward a set of French doors that had been throw open to the cool night breeze, he followed her. If she wanted fresh air, he'd accompany her, if only to engage her in conversation again. If things went well, he'd claim the kiss he'd thought about taking for days now. She'd barely gotten halfway across the wide terrace before he caught her up.

"It seems you and I both had the same idea. Taking in the night air."

Miss Bennett whirled around so quickly her sage green skirts flared about her ankles. Her eyes rounded as she stared.

"Mr. Ansley. I knew you'd arrived but hadn't had a chance to speak with you."

Intriguing. Did that mean he'd interested her? Geoffrey dared to step closer. As of yet, no one else had followed their lead and joined them. "Well, I'm here with you now. What's on your mind?"

She smiled, but it still didn't animate her face like he wanted. "Nothing except needing distance from the crowd in there."

"It looked to me as if you were enjoying yourself. You're quite popular." He inched close enough to lightly touch the inside of her elbow, a tiny bit above where the edge of her glove rested, then drew her nearer into the shadowy side of the terrace, away from the open doorway. He appreciated she didn't wear a shawl for warmth, for the bodice of the gown showed just enough creamy décolletage to entice him, as did a simple strand of pearls at her neck. She was a woman who didn't need added adornment. "You've not been without some love-sick pup hanging off your every word." Jealousy spiked through his gut, but he ignored it. There was no reason for such an emotion.

"Then you either weren't looking close enough or didn't see clearly. Crowds make me uncomfortable, and I certainly do not enjoy the attention, especially from men who I have no interest in." She peered at him from beneath her lashes. A pair of glittering combs nestling in her hair winked in the light of the nearly full moon. "So, tell me, why are you out here?"

"To speak with you." He had no reason to lie and less time for flirtation. At any moment, other couples or nosy dragons intent on propriety could exit the house.

"Oh?" She turned. Then with a tiny smile that stirred wicked thoughts in his brain. What would she do if he kissed her? She took his hand and led him deeper into the shadows. "Our conversation in my parlor didn't exactly invite another."

"That's because we were interrupted by the untimely arrival of your family, and then, when I attempted to speak with you in the bakery, the constable's son descended." That lout had almost made him boil over. He shoved thoughts of the unsavory man to dark recesses of his mind. Geoffrey drew Miss Bennett around. At least he could keep an eye on the door and make certain her back was to it. Hopefully, if they were disturbed, he could deflect attention before she was recognized, and her reputation put in danger. He dropped his voice. "I looked for you these last two days, but was thwarted each time."

"That would be hard to prove." She quirked an eyebrow. "Perhaps you should have tried harder."

"Indeed, on both counts." He grinned. Here in the dark, with the sharp chill of autumn all around them, the scent of bonfires in the air, and the buzz of laughter and conversation just inside, his daring grew. He cupped her cheek then slid his hand into her hair. The curls closed around his fingers like a living entity. "But luck is on my side now, and I have you all to myself. Will you grant permission for a kiss, Miss Bennett?"

Her eyes glittered. She wet her lips. "Out here?"

"Why not? It's a good a place as any for the moment." He made a show of looking around. The terrace was still private. "If the thought of kissing me scares you, I can withdraw my offer." Or maybe he wouldn't. He'd steal one anyway merely to banish the thought of doing so from his mind.

"No." She sucked in a breath then placed a hand on his chest. Geoffrey hissed as heat immediately seared that spot. "I mean, no, I'm not afraid of kissing you. In fact…" She tilted her head slightly to the right. "I've thought about doing so since I saw you in the hall… well, since I met you in that field."

The hall? "Now, that is very intriguing information." And he intended to delve deeper as soon as he could. His groin tightened as her lips tempted him. *I knew I hadn't mistaken that interest in her eyes before.* Geoffrey tugged her more firmly into his arms and slipped a hand to the small of her back. "It would be remiss of me to withhold something a woman as charming as you wanted."

"This is true." Miss Bennett's smile widened. "However, I will ask for one more concession."

"Anything." Impatience shot up his spine. If they delayed too much longer, they'd surely be found out.

She grasped one of his lapels. "Call me by my given name: Elinor. Miss Bennett is too formal and puts me in mind of being back in school."

"Is that what I call you when you've fantasized about this moment?" His voice was barely above a whisper as he lowered his head.

"Yes." Her breath warmed his cheek. "Except…"

"Except?" Why did he feel as if he hovered on a high cliff, ready to tumble off?

"I…" She never broke eye contact. "I've fantasized about you doing much more than kissing me." Her voice was so low, he nearly missed hearing the admission.

Damn and blast. His cock thickened. Did the woman have no idea about potential scandal? He didn't care. "Good." He crushed his mouth to hers then was lost in the wonder of Elinor Bennett.

Her lips were as soft as he'd hoped, but even as they welcomed him with a supple grace, it was obvious the woman had never been kissed before and had no experience in it. She simply stood there, crushing his lapel yet holding her head still, her mouth as unresponsive as a dead cod.

Geoffrey pulled slightly away. "Elinor, am I your first suitor?" His heartbeat thundered in his ears. Did he intend to be a suitor, or did he just want to steal a kiss on a darkened terrace?

"Yes." Her lips parted with a dreamy grin that had his cock pulsing with an insistent ache. "My first kiss as well. I'm on the shelf according to the gossips and never thought any man would want to kiss me, so—"

He cut off her rambles by kissing her again, and this time he applied himself to schooling the enchanting miss in the art of it. At first, he nibbled her bottom lip, letting her understand there was more to kissing than smashing one's lips against another's. Then he moved to tracing that silky lip with the tip of his tongue. When she gave a half giggle half sigh, he settled her more comfortably in his arms and deepened the connection. He teased the seam of her lips, hoping the glide of his tongue imparted the flutters every woman should experience upon their first kiss. Geoffrey pressed her closer, but the slight brush of his aroused length against her belly provided no relief and only set his blood on fire. As she opened slightly for him, at the last second, he refrained from turning the embrace too carnal. His body's reaction demanded an immediate halt to the proceedings lest he embarrass himself and her, but oh, how satisfying it would be to drag her off the terrace and find a secluded place in a darkened spot on the property. Instead, he glanced his tongue along hers, reveling in the warm satin, barely touching. Then he broke the kiss.

Elinor mewled a protest. She raised desire-laden eyes to his. "Why did you stop? That was wonderful."

"If I didn't, you and I would both be in trouble." His words sounded a tad breathless. He hadn't expected a kiss with a novice to shake him so much. Perhaps it was her red hair that he couldn't wait to see unbound and flowing about her shoulders or feel sliding along his skin. Or maybe it was her earlier talk of fantasies. *Damnation*. Whatever it was, he needed more time in her company. His engorged member pressed hard against the front of his breeches.

"I don't understand." She caught her bottom lip between her teeth in a gesture he was beginning to know betrayed her anxiety. "How will kissing do such a thing?"

With one last glance to be certain they were alone, his daring flew higher. "Just this." Quickly grabbing her hand, he pressed her palm to his aching cock then stiffened at her forced touch. *Stuff and bother*. He'd spend if he wasn't careful. It was a nodcock idea, introducing an innocent to something so scandalous, but being in Elinor's presence made him reckless. "You have to know at least some part of things if you dream of me doing them to you."

"Oh my." She sucked in a breath, blew it out then gently cupped his manhood and gave him the barest squeeze. "It feels just like it looked."

Like it looked? What the devil does that mean? Geoffrey put a decent amount of space between them, so that it wouldn't appear as if he'd compromised her, and to encourage his arousal to die down, yet the fleeting heat from her touch remained. "Yes, well, that is why we need to be careful. I don't want to embarrass myself or you." Plus, he needed to decide if he wished to court her. If he didn't, honor demanded he leave her alone else she'd be too much of a temptation. "I'd rather not rush you."

"Rush me into what, Mr. Ansley?" She started toward him, but he retreated, adamant about keeping them apart.

"Never mind. And please, do me the honor of calling me Geoffrey. I detest the formality just as you do." He shoved a hand through his hair. Somehow, the little minx had gotten under his skin and tormented his common sense. "Perhaps we should talk for the duration of our time together right now."

"About what?" Excitement edged her voice as she pursued him closer to the terrace wall.

Think, man. Make her talk about anything that doesn't pertain to the state of your cock.

"Tell me one of your darkest secrets." She must have some beyond what she'd already hinted at. The townsfolk wouldn't have said she was touched, otherwise.

That gave her pause. Elinor halted in the middle of the terrace. Now that she was nearer to the light from the doorway, her frown was fully visible. "I dream of doing something incredibly scandalous with a gentleman, something so big it will make me feel alive again, something beyond my fantasies."

"Feel alive? Are you not living right now?" Her way of speaking in vagaries intrigued him.

"I've felt dead inside since my friend Beatrice removed to London, perhaps long before that when I lost my family." Her expression shadowed as she moved away from the door.

"At least you cared for them—still do. Loving someone doesn't fade merely for the fact those people are no longer with us in whatever capacity."

"No." She shook her head. "I've learned there's no point in caring for someone because physical feelings—the ones that make my heart beat faster or my stomach warm—aren't emotions. They're merely temporal and they're much more real than emotions."

"Not quite, my girl. They're much the same, only emotions go deeper and engage us in our soul. They connect two people beyond what fleeting physical actions can do." What went on in her head that she was so conflicted?

"Perhaps I don't want to connect that way with someone again. It hurts too much, leaves emptiness behind." Her random pacing brought her to the doorway again. Tears sparkled in her eyes. "That's why I want a scandal to remember. It will make me feel but not engage me on a deeper level. It won't harm me."

"Oh, but you're wrong. Even a dalliance has the power to grab a person by their emotions, and with the right person, those can last longer than the affair." Poor thing. She had it all so lopsided, but he wanted to know more about her. "What then? You'll keep yourself warm at night with the memories of that scandal? You're still quite young with your whole life ahead of you."

"My age has nothing to do with how I feel." A hint of annoyance clung to her words.

"True, but why play the lead in a Gothic tale in your mind when you can make headway doing it in reality and enjoy yourself in the meanwhile." He rubbed a hand along his jaw. *I'd be as insane as she's reported to be if I choose to go down this path with her.* But she intrigued him beyond any other woman he'd ever known, and he wanted to begin the journey. "Perhaps you should take a chance on a man with a clouded pedigree and in the process find a bit of happiness you deserve in life." Shock speared his insides. Was that more or less a declaration?

"Is anyone out here? I thought I heard voices." The silhouette of a woman appeared in the doorway, backlit by candlelight, which delayed identification.

Geoffrey sprang back even more, though he wasn't anywhere near Elinor. "Yes, there are two of us out here. Miss Bennett and myself, Mr. Ansley."

"Ah." The woman joined them on the terrace. "I'm Lady Parker-Tarkington. Maggie to my friends, and I have a feeling we'll all be friends." She pinned her bright gaze on Geoffrey. "Is there a problem out here when you could be inside enjoying the party?"

"No, there is no problem. We were merely talking," Elinor mumbled.

"Taking in the air with less crowds," Geoffrey added. The name sounded familiar. He searched his mind for why, then it occurred to him. "You're married to Stephen. I met him in a pub a few days ago."

"Yes, I am. He's not as particularly fond of visiting as I am." Lady Parker-Tarkington laughed, and the gay sound echoed off the house. "I'm not as old or daft as you must think. A clandestine romance is all fine and good, but it has no place right here or now."

"I beg your pardon?" Geoffrey frowned. Would she accuse him and demand he offer for Elinor?

"Do it the proper way with accidental at-homes or meeting on empty lanes. The Surrey countryside is quite lovely this time of year, don't you think?" She winked at Geoffrey then addressed Elinor. "Miss Bennett, be a dear and fetch me a cup of punch. I'm quite parched." Once the redhead departed with nary a protest, Lady Parker-Tarkington continued, "Use your imagination if you wish to start a dalliance with the chit, but do have a care to stay out of the public eye. She's been through entirely too much as it is."

"I understand that." He sighed. "I'm unsure of how I wish to be with Elinor as my thoughts on the matter are rather muddled at present. I came to Surrey in order to covet the silence, as well as to study."

"I'm sure you did. Sometimes, fate throws people into our path, and we don't realize we were looking for exactly them." She patted his arm. "Just remember this. Will your reputation suffer more if you lead Elinor a merry chase into ruin, a girl who has just as many rumors following her as you do?"

"That is outside of enough. I won't have you maligning Elinor's reputation. From what I've ascertained, she's been unfortunate with luck. It's not her fault." He couldn't believe his gall in engaging the lady thusly, but the urge to protect Elinor took him by surprise. "Are you asking that I stay away from her?"

Lady Parker-Tarkington chuckled. She folded her hands at her waist. "Certainly not. My own romance started with a scandal. I am asking that you think things through. You can destroy much in a few minutes of pleasure that it might have taken years to build. Only you can decide which things are more important."

"I'll bear that in mind." He frowned as she returned to the house. The rustle of her silk skirts accompanied her. If she meant to warn him off Elinor, she had no idea of his mettle. There was no reason he couldn't enjoy both his reputation and a relationship with his pretty neighbor—in whatever capacity he deemed fit.

Chapter Five

Geoffrey drummed his fingers on his knees as he waited for an old acquaintance to make an appearance. The parlor where he'd been asked to wait was inside a modest house at one end of the village. Upon the advice of Mr. Adelaide, he'd begun calling on people he'd known during his school days, hoping they'd remember him as a boy and would be willing to put out a kind word or two about him within the community. If nothing else, it would be a good way to let on he'd be taking clients soon. As of yet, his reception had been less than warm. Of the people who had actually consented to receive him, most of them had glowing words to say about his father and brothers, and nothing but censure, disgust and warnings to give to him.

The sins of the father are being revisited by his son. Not that I've done anything wrong. I could not have helped which side of the blanket I was born on. Why should I have to pay for his crime?

Of course the rejection stung. Most likely it always would. No matter what he did, it would never be good enough because he was the result of an affair. Geoffrey's stomach clenched. Perhaps he should sell the property and return to New York, where no one cared about the circumstances of his birth or that he only held the Surrey property out of deathbed guilt.

Damn the English and their snobbery.

The one person who hadn't seemed to mind was Elinor—not that he'd told her his story. Undoubtedly, she'd heard the gossip already, but it might make a difference if he told her his version of being born on the wrong side of the blanket. He'd have to rectify the lapse, and soon. Not that they'd spent any time together beyond that brief visit on the terrace. It had been a couple of days since he'd kissed Elinor, and in that time, she'd occupied not only his waking thoughts but also his dreams. Why did he want to further a relationship with her, and in what capacity did he wish to know her? Had what Lady Parker-Tarkington said been a warning, or was she giving him permission to take the girl to bed?

He snorted. Not that Elinor was a girl. Oh no. The womanly curves that had pressed against his body were far from those of a girl. Thank the good Lord for that, for the thoughts he had of doing wicked things to her were only appropriate for someone above her majority.

"You have the look of someone lost in thought." A female voice cut through his musings. "I hope the subject of your attention is worth the effort."

Geoffrey slammed his gaze to the doorway where a woman entered. She was perhaps a few years younger than his thirty-two years, possessed masses of black, curly hair, and had a plain face and figure. He stood then turned to face the newcomer. "Hello. I'm Mr.—"

"I know who you are, Mr. Ansley," she answered for him. "My brother told me about you when we heard you'd come back to Surrey." She crossed the room and sat on one of the rose velvet wingback chairs. "I'm Martha, James' sister. I was a few years behind you in school, but I remember you tearing around the village and countryside with my brother and yours."

"Right, I remember you now." Geoffrey sat in a matching chair across a low table from hers. "I have fond memories of you and James." He gave her what he hoped was a disarming grin. "How have you kept yourself? Do you live here?"

"Yes, I live with James and his family since my husband died fighting Napoleon some years back." She nodded and returned his smile. "I enjoy looking after his children."

"Did he marry a local girl?" The last time he'd seen his friend James, they'd been ten-year-old boys more intent on playing pirates or knights in the country lanes than envisioning a future where they'd need to wed a female.

"No. He met her in London. Then when they married they chose to live in Surrey." Her brown eyes sparkled, but they weren't as pretty as Elinor's. "I take it that you've never wed?"

"No. The opportunity has never presented itself."

"I see." Martha's smile widened. "You may call on me if you'd like."

Before Geoffrey could answer and gently decline her offer, a man strode into the room. "Absolutely not."

"I beg your pardon?" Geoffrey stood. "James?"

"Yes." The man had the same curly black hair as his sister and the same brown eyes, as well as the frame of someone who enjoyed too much wine and rich food. In another ten years, he'd be portly with sagging jowls. "And you are Geoffrey Ansley, at least you were before you put on airs. Who do you tell people you are now?"

"I've hardly put on airs. The property was given to me. I had no say in it. It's merely a yoke around my neck instead of the sanctuary I wanted." Geoffrey hated that his tone had turned icy. Out of everyone he'd met with, he didn't think an old friend would treat him with such disrespect.

"No matter. Now that we know your real parentage, we can hardly welcome you into our home." James crossed his arms over his chest and glared.

"James, stop this nonsense," Martha pleaded. "Geoffrey and I were having a polite conversation. Would you like to join us?"

"No I would not." The man persisted in being surly. "I don't want to have anything to do with Geoffrey, or have even a trace of his name connected with ours." James strode to the door. "If you've gotten the idea to court my sister, you can think again. You're not fit to be in the same room as her."

A hot wave of anger swept through Geoffrey. "I merely came to pay my respects and to reminisce about old times with a friend. You and I grew up in each other's pockets. We were fast friends back then."

"We were, but you've talked enough. This visit is over." James' eyes shot daggers. "All of us liked the old earl well enough. We cannot have an upstart trying to undermine what his legitimate sons are doing for the area."

"Devil take it, that's a dim view of it, don't you think?" Of course, once again, the stigma of his birth was the only thing people would see. After this final blow, Geoffrey knew he wouldn't be able to escape the stories unless he completely washed his hands of England. "I thought you'd be receptive to me and would see I'm an upstanding man who just happened to have bad luck at birth."

A frown turned down James' mouth. "It's unfortunate, no getting around that, but think of my family's reputation.

Martha can still make a good marriage. She doesn't need you hanging about." He huffed. "Your mother lured the old earl to her bed. I cannot have you doing the same with my sister."

"James, for shame!" Martha interjected.

With a tight rein on his temper, Geoffrey curled one hand into a fist then just as quickly released it. *As if I'd follow in my mother's footsteps. No one ever saw that my father might have had a hand in passion taking over as well.* "Fine. I guess I was wrong about you and the bond we shared in childhood." No matter that he was a fine attorney or that he was a good man of manners and breeding, thanks to his mother's meticulous tutelage, the rumors and illicit conduct of his parents would always color him.

"I do apologize." James relaxed his rigid stance slightly. "I wish things were different."

"Not as much as I do, I'll wager." Geoffrey retrieved his outer garments from the table in the hall. "When, or if, you come to your senses, please feel free to call. Also, I am holding a rout at my manor on Guy Fawkes Night. I'm told it's customary to hold parties and such on this night as a celebration of sorts. I'd be pleased if you would come." Without a backward glance at the pair, he left the house. An olive branch extended was better than nothing.

That night, Geoffrey lay on his bed in the dark, still annoyed about the visit. So much for friendship. So much for wanting to make lasting connections in the community. Well, that would be his last try for a while. Starting tomorrow, he'd bury himself in his books, figure out what he needed to do in order to begin the process of practicing law in England, and he wouldn't care what went on in Surrey. It seemed he'd never outrun being a bastard and what it allegedly entailed. At least in England. Perhaps he should remove to America and bury his roots for good. Women wouldn't have anything to do with him here. Men feared what the reach of his reputation would do. What did it matter how—and to whom—he was born? Did being a good person and earning a modest living under his own power mean nothing? Except with Elinor. She was the bright, shining example. If he went back to New York, he wouldn't have her.

Restless and wide awake, he kicked off the bedclothes. The cool air rushed over his skin. His mind wandered back to the kiss with Elinor the night of Lady Parker-Tarkington's rout. The redhead had had the power to bring him to his knees then. If she'd been more experienced in kissing or seduction, he would have been unable to resist if she'd asked to remove to a more private location. Yet his mother's rules of conduct were instilled too deep. She'd been very adamant on how a gentleman deported himself, and that if a man had deviltry on his mind, he needed to be discreet and very certain the woman he dallied with agreed to everything—possible consequences as well.

If Elinor was indeed an innocent, he couldn't very well ruin her, not after he'd promised his mother he wouldn't be like his father.

Geoffrey gritted his teeth. What a damnable coil, especially since every thought of the woman made his shaft hard and aching. Even now, his erect cock tented his nightshirt and demanded attention. There was nothing for it except to pleasure himself and hope spending would send him into sleep. He yanked up the hem of the shirt, bunching the fabric at his waist then fisted his cock. A couple of strokes had him fully engorged and rampant. The slide of his thumb over the sensitive head provoked shivers of need through the length. A drop of moisture seeped from the slit, and he used it to lubricate the surface.

He thought of Elinor and how she'd squeezed him through his trousers on that terrace, how the touch of her fingers had sent fire into his blood, and he eased his hand down to the base where he fondled his balls, squeezing the stones, pretending it was her doing so. What would it be like to indulge her in carnal arts? Heat surged through him and shot into his cock. One stroke of his hand made the ache nearly unbearable. A second one intensified that feeling and had tingles teasing his flesh.

"Oh, God." He tightened his grip, moving his hand faster and with more urgency. An image of Elinor's smile floated into his mind and all he fixated on was her luscious lips and how they'd feel closed around his erection. Already he could feel every lick and twist of her tongue as she explored each hard inch of his length. He trembled at the mental pictures of her sucking hard on his aching member, coaxing his seed from his shaft and swallowing every drop he had to give. His belly tightened. His gut clenched. So close to bliss. Any second now he'd explode.

A moaning wail reached his ears, and it hadn't come from him. *What the devil was that?* A ghost in the walls? *I refuse to believe this house is haunted.* Still, his heartbeat pounded and it had nothing to do with pleasuring himself.

He shoved the interruption from his mind and continued to stroke his hand along his cock. Once. Twice. But his attention wavered, even more when the moaning came again, and this time it ended with a cry that sounded very much like a woman coming to sexual release.

"Bollocks." He couldn't spend with the racket in his walls. Geoffrey sprang from the bed. He paused long enough to light the oil lamp on the bedside table. Then, once weak golden light filtered through the room, he marched across the floor to where he'd last heard the sound.

A decided click echoed close by, followed by a sharp gasp. Damn it, he recognized that gasp. He'd bet his whole inheritance Elinor was behind that wall. But how? His erection flagged as he drew his fingers along the wall near the fireplace where he'd heard the sounds, searching for God only knew what. Seconds passed, marked by his thundering pulse and his rising annoyance. Then he felt a raised bump in the wallpaper. On a whim, he pressed it. A panel popped open, cleverly designed to match the paper's design, revealing a secret door.

"Damnation." Geoffrey caught the edge and pulled open the concealed door. Inside a darkened passageway, Elinor stood slumped against the back wall, an expression of bliss mixed with fear on her face, her eyes wide, and her glorious hair tumbling in waves about her shoulders. Her skirts were bunched and clutched in one hand, but he *knew* what she'd been about. She had the look of a woman recently sated. *Devil take it.* Had she pleasured herself behind his wall while watching him? As much as the knowledge brought him back to an aroused state, it didn't banish his earlier annoyance. "What the hell are you doing in here, and there'd better be a good explanation." Her disjointed rambles now made sense—seeing him in the hall, her comment that his member felt as good as it looked. "How long have you been spying on me?" After reaching inside the passage, he grabbed her wrist and yanked her into his room before being sure to swing the secret door closed behind her.

"I..." She licked her bottom lip then shivered. No wonder the chit was cold. She wore only a shift, a pair of thin slippers, and a gray woolen shawl. What the hell was she thinking traipsing about the countryside dressed like that? The urge to protect her, if even from herself, welled inside him, stronger than what he'd felt that day in her parlor when she recounted her history. "I've watched you since you moved in."

"The devil you say."

"Beatrice and I used the passages all the time. They connect this house to mine." Her shawl slipped down one shoulder to reveal the hard point of a nipple through the shift. "I didn't mean to continue, but when I saw you in the bath..." She visibly swallowed. "I couldn't contain my curiosity, and then, when I saw you pleasuring yourself again tonight, I did the same to my body and forgot to keep quiet."

"Hell's bells." Shock ricocheted inside him and landed deep in his member. All his manners and hopes of being a good, decent man flew out of his head when she lowered her gaze to his half-erect cock, clearly visible beneath the thin lawn of his nightshirt. Lust burned through his blood and collided with the recent slights and the violation of finding out that Elinor had spied on him during what should have been intimate moments.

"There are penalties for such behavior, my girl." Geoffrey pulled her closer to the bed. "If you spy and are found out, you might not enjoy your reckoning." Desperate to prove to himself he was still a man of substance, worthy of love and affection despite the circumstances of his birth, he spanned her waist with his hands. "Why did you come tonight, Elinor?" He softened his voice. There was still a chance he could do the noble thing and escort her back to her home without damage to either of their reputations. Such a thing depended upon his willpower and if he could keep his desire for her in check.

She laid both hands against his chest and the warmth of her skin blazed into his. "I hadn't seen you for two days, and since our kiss, I've been desperate for a glimpse of you. I've felt certain things for you, a madness of sorts."

If she hadn't looked at him from beneath her long lashes or caught her damn lower lip between her teeth, or had her voice not held a smoky quality that went straight to his groin, he would have bundled her up for home, and been happy to do so, but she had done all those things. And he adored every one of them. "I'll wager it's not madness that grips you when you let your fingers wander, but it is very, very naughty, and I intend to explore—perhaps even exploit—it."

Geoffrey brought his mouth to hers in a kiss designed to tell her, in no uncertain terms, that he was in control. He cajoled her lips apart and didn't wait for an invitation. Instead, he thrust his tongue inside to duel with hers. When she moaned and slid her hands up his chest to lock around his neck, he pulled her against him and plundered her mouth again and again, intent on dominating that silky organ. This time, the minx mimicked everything he did to her, and soon it was she who came perilously close commanding the embrace.

"It would seem you're a quick study," he murmured just before he tumbled them both onto his bed. Her red hair spilled around her like vibrant ink. His arousal pressed into her soft belly and set his blood aflame all over again.

"I never knew how wonderful kissing could be." She looped her arms around his shoulders, pulling him more firmly on top of her. "If I had, I would have endeavored to practice often."

"If you had done so, your reputation would be damaged beyond insanity." His mother's words rang in his head, but this time, he ignored them in favor of exploring Elinor. He drew his lips along the column of her throat then followed the neckline of the shift. Her skin smelled faintly of roses and was as soft as their petals. A sprinkling of freckles added a touch of whimsy. "As it is, I have no issue in teaching you the finer points of carnal play."

"Such as?" Elinor wriggled beneath him, and only succeeded in wedging herself tighter against him.

"Well, since it appears you're already skilled with finding your nub and bringing yourself to release," that in itself was welcome news as she would already have some clue about what went on between her thighs, "I shall have to find other ways to send you flying." He claimed her mouth in a bruising kiss then broke contact only to nibble a path down her chin and throat to meander over her collarbone. "You have a beautiful figure." The curves demanded his full attention, and he vowed he'd spend hours getting to know them soon. Geoffrey lifted off her body just enough that he could close his lips around one taut peak of a nipple. When she sucked in a quick breath, he chuckled then flicked his tongue over the tip, wishing her shift weren't in the way. He wanted to feel the pebbled texture, see what color it was when she was aroused.

"So do you." She slid her hands up and down his arms, and finally lingered at his shoulders, holding on.

"Men are not beautiful." He transferred his attention to the other nipple and lightly bit that one. At her moan, he took the tight bud into his mouth and sucked. Would that she was completely naked, but it wasn't much of a problem. There were ways of pleasuring a woman even with some manner of clothing on. He pulled away and looked into her face. A faint smile curved her lips. Her eyes sparkled in the lamplight. His cock twitched. "Aren't you a delectable piece all laid out beneath me?" He nestled his arousal into the valley between her thighs. Only the thin cotton of her attire prevented his length from penetrating her heat. God, he needed a distraction or else he'd take full advantage of her right now.

Elinor dug her fingers into his upper arms. "Oh, I like that. Rub yourself against me again." She tilted her hips and his balls, still enclosed by his nightshirt, glanced along her fabric-covered folds. "Mmm."

If she kept up her innocent demands and sounds of enjoyment, he'd spend all over himself. Damn it, he'd much rather do so inside of her and show her exactly why bringing oneself to release was not as good as having a partner. "I think you'll like this instead." Geoffrey slid down her body and off the bed until he knelt on the floor.

She levered onto her elbows. "What are you about?"

"Showing you something shocking." He grabbed her legs and pulled her to the edge of the mattress. The shift bunched and rolled beneath her, revealing pale legs and silky skin. "Perhaps this will be your scandal." Once in position, he spread her thighs wide. "I revise my earlier statement of beautiful." Fully on display and framed by fiery red curls, her folds bloomed and opened, pink and glistening with moisture. "You are gorgeous, Elinor." *And so very tempting.* His mouth watered in anticipation.

"Men enjoy seeing a woman's nether bits?" Surprise laced her voice.

"Don't be coy, my girl. Did you feel lust or desire when you saw my naked member?" His body burned still at the thought she'd watched him secretly.

"Yes." She whispered the word.

"Then yes, of course, men like to see a woman's flower. The sight of those folds sets our blood on fire and ignites passion." Geoffrey inhaled the faint musk of her arousal. His cock tightened, but he ignored his building need. "Plant your feet on the bed." Once she did as instructed, he swiped his tongue along her sex. Her tart sweetness exploded on his palate and fired his lust. Her damp curls grazed his cheeks.

"Oh!" Elinor wiggled. He gripped her ankles. "I never knew..." Her words trailed off as he licked her folds again, this time with greater pressure. "Dear heavens that's wonderful."

He chuckled and hoped she felt the vibrations against her flesh. Over and over, he lapped and nibbled her soft flesh, and when she trembled, he closed his lips around her swollen button, sucking it into his mouth then teasing the captive bud with his tongue.

She squirmed. One of her legs slipped from the bed and fell over his shoulder. Geoffrey moved closer. He kept her in the cycle of nipping, licking, sucking, and soothing, his tongue and mouth constantly busy until her whimpers turned into panting cries. "Mr. Ansley. Geoffrey. I feel the madness descending." Need punctuated her statement.

"Damnation, woman, it's not madness." He tightened his hand around her ankle. "It's perfectly natural. Never let anyone tell you otherwise." He wanted to see her come to release, desired to hear the sounds she made when she spent. "Fall over that edge for me. Give in to what your body tells you." He nipped at her engorged nub, flicked his tongue back and forth over it. As she shuddered and fisted the bedclothes, he pulled slightly away then blew on her wet folds.

Elinor whimpered. "Almost there."

Stubborn girl. Why wouldn't she just let go now since she'd apparently found it so easy in his wall? Geoffrey applied himself to the task with greater resolve even as his cock grew hard to the point of pain. When he suckled her button, he stroked his free hand along his shaft. The touch gave small relief and nothing short of burying his length in her heat would do.

He penetrated her warm channel with his tongue, thrusting over and over, coating it in her juices, but it was a poor substitute for the real thing. He imagined her wetness clinging to his member as he slid in and out, and he grew even harder. Still, the fevered play was the added incentive she needed, for Elinor shattered with a hoarse cry of surprise. Her back arched. She dug her heel into his shoulder, forcing him closer. Geoffrey lapped at the tangy juices spilling from her channel before pulling away. When her leg on his shoulders relaxed, he scrambled to his feet and caught the expression of bliss on her face. Her eyelids fluttered closed while a soft smile curved her lips. His stomach clenched with raw need.

"Elinor." He leaned over her, and his erect, pulsing cock scraped against the fabric of his nightshirt. Sensation streaked along his skin and nearly sent him over, even more so when his tip bumped her wet opening, but he gritted his teeth. "Have you lain with a man before?" Despite her affinity for carnal pleasure, he was fairly certain she was a virgin.

"No," she gasped and opened her eyes. "Will you teach me that too?"

Devil take the circumstances and his common sense. Disappointment flooded him like a blast of cold water.

"Not tonight." In the end, he couldn't forget the gentleman he was raised to be. A bitter laugh escaped him. Perhaps he should give into his fate and be as wicked as the rumors said he was simply because he was born on the wrong side of the blanket. He crawled up the bed beside her and collapsed onto his back. His erection tented his nightshirt, mocking him. "I cannot in good conscience besmirch your reputation for the mere fact that I never had the chance to own mine." He stroked a hand through her ribbons of hair tangled on the bed. "You're too much the innocent and can still redeem yourself."

His chest tightened and disenchantment slid down his spine. Never had a decision been so difficult to make, but he was certain on one point—he'd have to board up her access to the passageways inside his home. If she wanted to watch him, she could damn well ask permission first.

Chapter Six

Elinor shivered with the residual bliss from the release Geoffrey had given her. He'd willingly touched her, done intimate things to her without provocation. Perhaps she wasn't as undesirable as she'd thought. A smile tugged at her lips. It had been so much more wonderful than touching herself. *He brought me to release.* By his mouth no less, yet she didn't feel fulfilled. Deep inside, her core pulsed, needing something more she couldn't name. She pushed herself up the mattress until she lay on her side next to him. Where had he learned such a skill and why did the thought of him pleasuring other woman the same way cause her throat to tighten?

She wet her lips and glanced at him. Shadows from the flickering lamp flame moved over his face. He kept his gaze fixed on the ceiling, and she studied him while her breathing returned to normal. He'd been so angry and shocked when he'd discovered her in the secret passage. She'd had no idea what he would do. She should have been embarrassed he'd found out her secret, but seeing him with such passion and determination in his eyes had left her speechless, even more so when he'd pulled her into his room and pleasured her. How far would he go if she goaded him?

"Say what you mean to say. It is quite disconcerting and rude for you to keep staring at me," he grumbled, but he tucked his hands behind his head and didn't move away from her.

Before she could change her mind, Elinor rested a hand on his stomach, pleased when he tensed beneath her fingertips. She eyed his flagging member, not as proudly erect as it had been moments before. Did she move him the same that he did her? If she did, why did his arousal fade? "Why do you think you cannot be a good person despite the rumors? There is always gossip. It's either true or not, and if it isn't, why should you care?"

"Good question." He frowned as if he were unhappy with the shadow-shrouded ceiling. "The problem? The gossip is mostly true. I cannot help that I was born a bastard, raised in the same house of my privileged brothers. Because it's true, I'm forced to acknowledge it and cannot ignore it."

"Then you should be used to it, as it's your history. Why not work around it?" Just being in the same bed with someone as handsome as he kept her in a state of high sensitivity. Her hard nipples poked against her shift and shivers shot down her spine and the awareness reminded her of his mouth on them. Did he not feel as affected?

"I'm trying. Don't you understand?" Finally, he looked at her. Annoyance and sadness mixed in his eyes. "I'm trying. Why do you think I'm making the rounds of the gentry as well as my past acquaintances? Besides, it doesn't matter as it makes no difference. The man I am will never overcome my birth or the fact my father gave me the property to assuage his guilt as he lay dying."

"Then why try to impress the notables? Work on the common people, the folks in the pubs and fields. They're the honest folk, the ones who will support your cause, especially if you wish to be a solicitor here in Surrey. They'll be who you'll labor for."

"How did you become so wise about the workings of humanity?"

"I don't know how wise I am. I have my fair share of problems and secrets. Secrets that now you know." The fresh, clean scent of him teased her nose and made her feel comforted, as did the easy way they both reclined. "Tell me about your childhood. If it's preying on your mind so much, give words to the thoughts." She slid her hand up his chest. The heat of his body warmed her fingers and she wished she were smashed against his form instead of lying next to it.

He cocked an eyebrow. "Perhaps you're right." A sigh escaped him. "My mother was an American. So, you and I have the land of your birth in common."

"That, and we're both outcasts from highborn British society."

"True."

"Not to sound crass, but when did your mother commence the dalliance with the old earl—before or after she became employed within the household?" The story was fascinating in its scandal but sad just the same. So many lives changed due to passion.

"From what I've been able to piece together, she was the boys' governess for a year before she and the old earl started up."

Elinor frowned. "And no one questioned her pregnancy? That should have been suspect at the very least."

His eyes lit. "You are quite astute. I'll have to be careful around you." He tapped the end of her nose. "Apparently, when Mother discovered she was with child, she hid the evidence as best she could. From what she told me, the task was easy as she didn't show for months. Not even the servants knew, though a couple of them suspected. There were rumors." He shrugged, and the movement caused his nightshirt to pull at his shoulders. "Midway through the pregnancy, she went away. She'd told the earl she was visiting her relatives in America, which was good in a way. Even still, the earl took his family off on their own holiday to Ireland and onward to Scotland. I'm told they were away for months."

"But she didn't go to America?"

"No. She retired to a cottage the earl had bought for her near Bath and gave birth to me there. By that time, the earl had taken his family to London to enjoy the Little Season after their holiday." Geoffrey cleared his throat. "She returned to her post without me."

"I beg your pardon?" Elinor's chest constricted. What sort of a woman abandoned her newly born child to come back to the house of the man who used then abandoned her?

"The one time she told me the story, she said she went back to her post without me."

"I'm so sorry." She grabbed one of his hands and held it to her cheek in the hopes of comforting him.

"Silly girl, it was thirty-two years ago. Those wounds aren't fresh any longer." He switched their hand positions then pressed a fleeting kiss to her palm. "But fate isn't a mistress to trifle with. Though my mother had dewy-eyed dreams of being more to the old earl, he didn't share that view. Their affair dwindled. Two years later, the woman who Mother had paid to take me died. When they found her body, her family discovered a note pinned to my clothing, saying I belonged to Mother."

"So you ended up living with the old earl anyway." Elinor couldn't stifle her giggle. "Did your mother let on that your two-year-old self was her flesh and blood?"

"No. The story she'd told me, as well as everyone else, was that I came from one of her distant cousins who died unexpectedly and had no other family. For whatever reason, the earl's household accepted the excuse. Maybe they turned a blind eye to his indiscretions. I don't know."

She squeezed his hand before releasing it. "Not a very auspicious start to life, but you did all right for yourself." When she held his gaze, her stomach flipped at the intensity in his. "There's nothing to be ashamed about."

"Thank you for that." His heavy sigh stirred a lock of his hair that tumbled over his forehead. "I think at the time, I assumed since she was my brothers' governess, she was mine too." His sensual mouth curved with a small grin. "My earliest memories are of being with my two older brothers, running amok through our country estate or going up to London and enjoying the city." He swallowed and his Adam's apple bobbed. "However, when I turned eight, I distinctly remember my brothers going away to school. My mother and I saw them off as they boarded the earl's coach one day. It occurred to me that I wasn't going and I asked her why. I had no idea then, but knew there was something inherently wrong, regardless that

I wasn't the same station of the boys. To my childish way of thinking, we were all equals."

Elinor's stomach trembled. She could well see where the story would go. "Oh no."

"It is what it is." Geoffrey tucked a strand of hair behind her ear. "She comforted me as the coach pulled away. She said I was too smart for that crumbling, snotty school and that God must have better things ahead for me."

"Sound advice. You must take after her."

He traced a finger along her cheek. "Careful, my dear. I could come to adore a woman who says such pretty things like you do."

Did he truly mean those words or were they merely part and parcel of the charming gentleman he'd perfected? No matter, her pulse kicked up with the contemplation.

He continued his caress and moved his palm over her shoulder and down her arm. "But that's how she was, always so comforting and warm. She knew just what to say to stem my tears and helped ease the nasty things my brothers would say to me because I was smarter than them."

"How did you find out the truth?" Elinor stifled a moan as he moved to her hip then began a return trip. Being in bed with a man, having him touch her, was both discomfiting and altogether a wonderful experience.

"Two years later, I was at the market with my mother. A couple of women asked her to buy their wares. When Mother refused, the women made a couple of rude comments about her putting on airs just because she'd cuckolded the earl and had his child. My mother denied the stories, but the women kept on, and soon rumors made their way around the village.

They eventually reached the ears of the earl's wife, and she confronted him about it. He didn't deny the story, so she turned my mother and me out immediately."

"How horrible." Elinor knew how hard it was to find employment with rumors nipping at the heels. The only reason she'd landed her spot in the bakery was from imploring old Mrs. Colfax and by showing her a sample of what she could actually bake: cinnamon buns. Not only that, but also most folks had refused to give her a spot since her station was above that of a common laborer. It had annoyed her that she couldn't work at a trade she enjoyed for the mere circumstances of her worth.

"It's how things are done in the *ton*." He looked so vulnerable stuck in those memories that she scooted closer to him and played her fingers along his jaw line. "We rented a room in the village inn while Mother figured out a plan. A courier came later that night with a packet of clothing for both of us and enough money that Mother could start over somewhere far away from Surrey if she wanted."

"From your father?"

"I assume so. It was anonymous. Mother never really talked much about him or their relationship."

"Why did your mother come to England to begin with? It seems up to chance if she came looking for employment. There should have been plenty in America."

"Honestly? I never did get that part of the story. Suffice it to say, Mother's secrets apparently went deep and were vast. From what I managed to piece together, she'd been struck by wanderlust and arrived with a cousin." He shrugged. "After my brothers left for school, she took me to America and her family."

Elinor snorted. "And they didn't have words for the return of a prodigal daughter with a child in tow?" What a coil that must have been.

"She told me she invented a marriage that ended in tragedy. I never inquired further since I trusted her even though most of her explanations could be lies. I regret I didn't push for the full story." He rubbed a hand over his face. "But, America was far enough away that she could start over in New York." He pinned her with a look that brimmed with hope. "In my heart of hearts, I'd like to believe he loved her at one time and that's why he had the affair and why he let her continue to live in his house even after I was born."

She brushed the lock of hair back from his forehead. "Do you think he knew?"

"Perhaps. I don't look very much like Mother. I never saw the old earl enough to study how we might be alike. I just know he never singled me out nor did he pay any overt attention to me." Geoffrey caught her wrist in his hand then trailed a line of feather-light kisses down the sensitive inside of her arm. "Have I scared you away with that convoluted tale?"

"No." She couldn't think clearly, since the shivers he'd invoked increased with each new brush of his lips. "But then, your story is no different than hundreds of other people over the whole of England. I'm sure there are bastards in more places and positions than you'd like to think."

He reared back on the bed, so they no longer touched. "How ironic you'd say that since your current history is less than ideal." Hurt shadowed his expression. "For me, it's my life and how I started. I refuse to be defined by it or lessened because of it."

"Except you're using your birth circumstances as an excuse for why Surrey won't accept you. Who cares if the titled and over-privileged look down their long noses at you? Show them why you're better than them despite your lineage." She struggled into a sitting position. "If I've offended you, I'm sorry, but I fail to see how being a bastard would affect you one way or the other. Build your life on who you are now and what you have to offer the world."

"Do not presume to tell me how I should feel or look at the situation." Ice fairly dripped from his words as he knelt on the bed.

"I'm not." She folded her legs. Anxiety crawled over her skin. With his flashing eyes and the hard set of his jaw, he'd gone from charming to formidable in mere seconds.

"You are." He narrowed his eyes. "How can you even think to counsel me when you spend so much time ignoring the hurt in your own life?"

"I haven't—"

Geoffrey held up a hand. "Spare me the empty excuses." He shook his head. "You go through life keeping people at arm's length in an effort not to be hurt. You spend your time spying on others, watching them do the things you wish you could have the courage to do, always on the outside looking in but never being an active part of your own life. Why?"

Her heartbeat accelerated. It pounded in her ears and hammered in her tight chest. "I don't keep people away. They willfully give me a wide berth." Even as she said the words, she knew they weren't true. Outside of Beatrice, she'd made a point to only interact with the villagers in polite but standoffish ways, a few words at the bakery or market, a passing hello in the lane. She never accepted invitations, and eventually, no one bothered to invite her to their homes or parties anymore.

"I'll wager you do. Again, I ask why? Is it because you're afraid to let someone love you due to feeling unworthy, or are you terrified that you'll love someone, and they'll leave you?" He dropped his voice. "Either way, it's no way to live."

"Is that so? This from the man who battles his own low self-worth." Her chest heaved from the force of her breaths that should have calmed, but didn't.

"That is beside the fact." His nostrils flared. "Why wouldn't you want to immerse yourself in a full range of emotions? If you're hurt, you'll feel it and know you're alive, have a benchmark and a goal to do better next time."

"Do better next time? How, pray tell, when all the members of my close family are dead?" She frowned as her mind spun. Why did he have to be logical? Why couldn't he just be a typical, stoic, stiff upper-lipped Englishman who'd rather die than talk about emotions? Elinor stifled a sob. She unfolded her legs and attempted to scramble off the bed, but she caught a foot in the hem of her shift.

"That's not what I meant."

"Well, let me tell you what I think of love, and risk or bravery." She untangled herself then scooted toward the edge of the bed, her shift bunching and rolling beneath her. "They're wasted emotions. Why should I let myself love someone? They *will* leave and I'll be hurt and alone." To her horror, hot tears sprang to her eyes. She'd refused to cry after the tragedies of her family, and she wouldn't do so now. "I have overwhelming evidence of that. I won't put myself in that position again."

"It's called experience, my girl. No one gets to skip through life knowing only happiness and bliss. Imagine how trying that would be after a while." He reached for her, but she twisted away, sliding off the bed and landing on unsteady legs. "You have to balance the good with the bad."

"No, I don't." She whipped around until she faced him. He adjusted on the bed. She jabbed a finger into his chest. "Don't presume *you* know what's best for *me*. I'm protecting myself."

"Are you, or is it all one big lie you have to tell yourself just to make it through a day without breaking down and letting yourself grieve?" Though his voice was still low, intensity rang in it, and his eyes had darkened to green pools, intense in the lamplight.

"What does that mean?" Her anger and annoyance died in the face of new emotions crowding in the longer he looked at her with that hungry gaze.

"What will it take for you to feel again, to experience something so deep in your soul you have to cry out and embrace it, acknowledge it, lest it strangle you, then be grateful that it happened because you learned something?" Geoffrey grabbed her arm and pulled her into his lap. "You told me days ago you wanted a scandal. Will that be the catalyst that brings you back from the dead?"

"I'm not dead." And he wasn't either if the insistent poke of his erect cock against her bottom was any indication. "Don't be daft." Heat slid through her insides to center in her core, and she squirmed which only ground his length harder into her backside.

"You are, hiding yourself away in your house, never venturing out except to spy on me." He held her chin between his thumb and forefinger. "What are you afraid of, Elinor?"

She wrenched her chin out of his grip, unable to stand the interest in his eyes or the reaction of her body to him. "I don't want to care, to hurt, to watch another person in my life go away. I cannot bear to know that my being in their lives isn't enough to keep them with me. It has to be me who causes all the ill luck, don't you see? Because they all leave, except that weasel Nigel. For whatever reason, he's still here." A laugh escaped, but it sounded more like a hysterical sob. She swallowed it and blinked away her tears. Geoffrey didn't care about her silly ramblings, but when she wriggled in his hold, he refused to release her.

Several silent seconds slid by. She kept her focus on the rumpled bedclothes while he rubbed a hand up and down her arm. Finally, he dumped her off his lap then stood.

"And I cannot bear knowing a woman of my acquaintance thinks so little of herself that she's shut herself away to guard her heart from an event that may never happen." Geoffrey knelt. He lifted one of her feet, removed the slipper then did the same to the other foot. Once he stood, he gripped her shoulders and gave her a little shake. "If nothing else comes of you slinking through passageways and watching me in intimate moments, let it be this: I will teach you that actually living your life won't hurt you and that caring about another person won't destroy you, but instead will make you stronger and able to face each new day with confidence and appreciation."

She gasped at the fierce passion in his voice. Why did it matter so much to him what became of her? "What bearing does any of this have on you?"

"Just this." With a smile brimming of wicked intent, he pulled the shift up and off her body in one fell swoop then dropped it on the floor. "My father didn't seem to care about my mother or any of the problems she found herself in. He didn't care about me when I lived under the same roof as him. He didn't care when the gossipmongers tore my mother's reputation to shreds or when his real sons bullied me. And he most certainly didn't care about either of us when he died. The gifts he bestowed on me were to make him feel better, not to ensure my future or well-being."

"I don't understand." How could she when he talked of feelings and life but undressed her at the same time? A shiver danced down her spine, but it had nothing to do with the chill in the room or the fact she was now naked in front of him. When she moved to cover her breasts with her hands, he shook his head.

"Do not hide yourself." Geoffrey removed his nightshirt and stood as naked as she. The garment joined her clothing on the floor at their feet. His member, proud and rampant, bobbed with the movement. "I want you to know that I am not the same sort of man my father was."

"Even a blind woman would know that." Her head felt heavy and full of wool. Why couldn't she figure out his motives?

He grinned. "Yes, well, I refuse to see another woman in my circle fade away from guilt or false hope to excuse what has happened to her."

A revelation plowed into Elinor chest with enough force to weaken her knees. "Your mother is dead, isn't she?"

"Yes." The one word held so much sorrow and grief she swore she felt it in her own chest. "She wasted away, pining after the rogue who fucked her then left her to weather life's storms alone. Not even my faith in her or love for her could recall her from the brink. She left me just as your family left you. I'm stronger for it. You should be too."

She bit her bottom lip. Her ears rang from his vulgarity while her mind reeled at what was about to play out. "And sleeping with me will somehow make the situation better?"

"Oh, my girl, it won't make anything better, and will greatly complicate everything, but I can no longer deny the demands of my body, for you are quite the tempting package."

"But—"

"Hush. I know you feel the connection between us, that pull, that heat," he interrupted. "I see it in your eyes, but I promise you this." He picked Elinor up into his arms and lightly tossed her onto the bed. Her breasts bounced as she landed, and he followed the movement with his gaze. "I will stand by you through the consequences, no matter what happens. I might break my vow of being a gentleman tonight, but I won't tomorrow morning."

Another round of shivers skated over her skin. "I don't need your pity." Did he feel sorry for her, or worse, want to save her because he couldn't save his mother? "Don't replace your mother with me. We are not the same people. Plus, things between you and I would be too weird if that were so."

"I know you're not. I'd never want you to be. She was silly and chased impossible dreams. You are strong, even if you don't think it of yourself." Geoffrey joined her on the mattress, covering her body with his bigger, more solid one, and held her gaze. "But you are very much a maiden in distress, now even more so than when I rescued you from the evil Nigel, and if I can save you from a fate worse than him, I want to try."

Her heart trembled and she smiled, though it was tremulous at best. "Because you are a gentleman?"

"Absolutely." He smoothed a lock of wayward hair from her brow. "Do you trust me?"

"Yes." Never had she been given such consideration before, let alone from a man she barely knew, or a man at all. Tears crowded her throat, preventing her from uttering more appropriate words. So she did the next best thing. She held his face between her palms and kissed him, putting every ounce of gratitude and bewilderment she felt in into that one meeting of mouths.

He groaned low in the back of his throat and returned the kiss. When he moved his lips over hers, she opened her mouth, inviting him in as he'd shown her earlier. The second he touched his tongue to hers, she matched him thrust for thrust. In that one, perfect moment, she didn't need words, didn't need anything else except the feel of his solid body on top of hers and the warmth of his tongue as he explored the inside of her mouth. She slid her arms around his broad shoulders and held him as close as she could.

"Geoffrey." She murmured his name against the side of his neck. Then the corded muscle there occupied her full attention, and she kissed a path to his shoulder. The insistent nudge of his arousal sat between her thighs, a constant tease that she couldn't wait to feel inside her.

"Mmm?" He nibbled on her earlobe. "Is there something you want, my girl?"

Elinor sighed in a passion-filled haze. "Love me." Would he read too much into what she'd asked? Did she want him to? "I mean..." A flush swept over her skin. Was she too inexperienced for him?

"I know what you mean." He held his weight on his forearms and looked down at her. "It will go quick. I'm near my limit as we speak. Have been since you apparently watched me pleasure myself earlier this evening." With a knee, he urged her thighs apart.

"I'll enjoy it regardless." She wriggled into a more comfortable position beneath him. A host of tingles chased through her core as the head of his cock kissed her opening then waited there, teasing, just dipping shallowly in and out. "Do it soon. I'm not very good at being patient."

Geoffrey nipped the underside of her jaw, and the scrape of his stubble against her skin loosed flutters in her belly. "We cannot all be patient." He claimed her lips in a long, drugging kiss and at the same time, he pushed into her passage and didn't stop until he was fully sheathed.

A sting of sharp pain swamped her when he took her maidenhead. Elinor caught her breath and stilled. She dug her fingernails into his shoulders. "Oh."

A long groan left his throat. "And I am not patient where you're concerned.

"Somehow, I'm glad for it." She released her held breath as she wriggled her hips, making his passage easier.

I'm sorry I've hurt you. It will be easier during subsequent times." He withdrew and she whimpered at the immediate loss of his heat.

"Then this isn't an impromptu session we won't repeat?" She hated how hope filled her heart. It would lead to only disappointment later.

"I rather doubt it." Geoffrey returned to her channel, and the moisture coating her folds hastened his movements. He moaned, pausing. "If you want the scandal, I'm volunteering for the position." A wicked grin curved his mouth. "Perhaps I won't have that passageway boarded quite so soon after all. It's thrilling to know we can sneak back and forth for the specific purpose of carnal games."

"Why, Mr. Ansley, how positively naughty..." The rest of her sentence dissolved once he found a rhythm, and each thrust loosed a host of pleasurable sensation within her core. "Oh my."

"Meet me." He slid his hands beneath her bottom and lifted her. "Move with me. I won't last."

Elinor applied herself to the task, and after a few awkward attempts, she moved her hips in time with each push. Each crash of their bodies intensified the feelings. Pressure built inside her. It grew larger and filled her body with a need she didn't fully understand. It was similar to what she felt when fingering her nub, but bigger, grander, with the potential of consuming her.

"Good God, please say you're near." Strain ravaged his voice. His arms shook as he penetrated her. "I won't finish without you."

What sort of man was he that he considered her needs along with his? From all the stories she'd heard from women in the village or the maids, men found release; then the act was over. She swallowed around the lump of tears in her throat. "I am." In order to hurry things along, she slipped a hand between them then strummed her fingers over her swollen, slippery button. Tremors circled through her lower belly. Her attention, coupled with Geoffrey's ministrations, sent her tumbling over the edge into bliss moments later. A moan escaped from her lips.

He thrust once more and with a gasp, he hit his own release. He pulled out and the warm ropes of his seed emptied onto the bed at her hip. When he collapsed upon her, she merely wrapped her arms around his waist and held him. His heartbeat raced in time with hers, his breath warm at her temple.

"Why did you move off me at the last moment?" Never had the maids whispered of such a thing, or if they did, she hadn't listened.

"I didn't wish to repeat the sins of my father."

Her heart squeezed. "Yet you said you'd be a gentleman for me in the morning, come what may."

"I did, and perhaps the next time we share our bodies, I'll give you everything." He pressed a kiss to her temple. "Thank you for that gift. I'll strive to cherish it."

She burrowed her face into the crook of his shoulder as tears prickled her eyes. "I believe you." It was appalling how desperately she wished to mean something more to him than a bed partner. But, until she knew more about him, she'd have to be sure to guard her heart against him in case he was good on his word.

Chapter Seven

Geoffrey laid down his pen at a minute before midnight. For hours his studies had consumed his attention. The laws of Britain were not much different than those of America. It would take no time at all before he'd be ready to befriend a noted man in the field and perhaps ask for an apprenticeship if he couldn't take the exams and start a practice alone. The thought triggered a sigh. Helping people unravel their legal knots was where he'd be most comfortable. Perhaps Elinor had been correct. He needed to court the common people's favor instead of the gentry's. After all, he would be working for the people. He vowed to do the rounds of pubs and public houses, share a meal with the regular folk and start to make inroads there.

He stood, gave into a leisurely stretch then took up the oil lamp and exited his study. The house stood silent and shrouded in darkness—to the uninitiated eye. Yet, he knew, somewhere within the secret passageways Elinor lurked, watching him. The thought curved his lips into a smile. He could almost feel her presence, the naughty girl. As he slowly climbed the stairs, his grin widened. It had been two nights since his relationship with her had tumbled into the carnal, and though they hadn't been together last night, he'd been surprised he'd missed her.

He'd enjoyed exchanging conversation with her a little more than he should have, but had adored initiating her into the ways of carnal delights even more. Now, the hairs on his nape prickled.

She's here, watching me this very instant. His pulse accelerated. He gripped the lantern's handle more firmly, willing it not to shake and betray his excitement. Was she here to merely spy on him or did she desire a turn in his bed?

As much as he wanted to pelt up the stairs to his bedroom, he forced himself into some semblance of calm and strolled along the corridor until he reached the staircase. Once there, he dutifully climbed them as if he had all the time in the world. Was she wearing a shift like the last time or was she fully clothed? The mere thought that she lurked in his walls hardened his shaft.

He chuckled. *I had no idea England would be so delightful.*

By the time he gained his suite and had closed the door behind him, he couldn't stand the suspense. He had definite plans for the unusual woman and couldn't wait to employ them. Would she object to a bit of deviant behavior during a sexual romp? Only time would tell, but he liked to think she'd be game for anything, especially since she had a definite penchant for pleasuring herself in his walls. After quickly setting the lamp onto the bureau top, Geoffrey crossed the room, pressed the correct spot on the wall then waited as the panel popped open. His heart lurched when he found the passageway beyond dark and empty. What the devil? He couldn't have been wrong. The prickles he'd felt weren't imagined.

One stride carried him into the passageway, and he immediately wrinkled his nose against the scent of dust and the damp. The lantern's light didn't reach far into the corridor, yet the harder he peered into the gloom, the more he perceived a sort of bouncing illumination. Squinting didn't provide new information, so he waited as his heart beat out of control and chills played his spine. Closer and closer the golden light came. Only when it was nearly upon him could he finally ascertain what it was. Elinor held a candle, shaded with a hand in front of it, looking for all the world as if she'd raced the whole way.

Scraps of cobwebs clung to wisps of her flyaway red hair and a pretty blush stained her pale cheeks. "I had intended to already be in your bed and waiting, but I encountered a rat on my way here and no amount of shooing would persuade it to move along." She shuddered. "I didn't wish to step over it in case it pounced."

A sigh of relief left his throat. "My girl, I don't believe rats pounce." He blew out her candle, grabbed her free hand and pulled her into his bedroom. Once she was safely inside, he closed the panel. "I worried you wouldn't come." He tamped his anticipation. It wouldn't do to give too much away so early in the relationship.

"Believe me, I wanted to come last night, but my uncle demanded I attend a dinner party at the Underhill home. He has dreams of me making a match with one of the baron's sons." Elinor deposited her candle on the bureau. "It was a long and trying evening with Lady Underhill attempting to prevent me from talking with her sons and the baron introducing new topics of discussion, along with my uncle, to encourage conversation between me and the men."

"Oh? Does either of those men interest you?" His chest tightened at the thought of losing her to someone else. As he raked his gaze along her body, he couldn't help but see the naked curves that were hidden beneath the staid, gray wool dress and a truly horrible, tattered black shawl. No, he didn't like the idea of Elinor with someone else by half, not when he'd just found the treasure that she was.

Her eyes danced with mischief. "The Underhill boys? Absolutely not. They're great, hulking men whose brains are buried beneath the pudding between their ears."

"I'm glad to hear it." Geoffrey relaxed. "Well, to hear that you don't favor them, not that they have pudding in their heads. They must be such a disappointment to their parents." He grinned, not having yet had the pleasure of meeting any of the Underhill clan.

An answering grin pulled at the corners of her mouth. "I don't know if Lady Underhill realizes her sons aren't the paragons of virtue she thinks they are, while the baron is anxious to shove them off his hands. Honestly, I think they're too expensive to keep feeding." She broke into peals of laughter that animated her face and smoothed the lines of worry from her brow. "Uncle, bless his heart, hasn't given up and still pushes me at them."

"I assume you've told him neither of those men will suit?"

"Of course." She shook her head. "He's desperate to match me."

"Why?" Another surge of jealousy went through Geoffrey's gut. Would his dalliance with her end because she found herself engaged to another thanks to the overzealous machinations of her uncle? He frowned. He wasn't ready to give her up. Something about her begged for greater understanding and he wanted to be the man to unlock her heart, be her key, the only thing she'd ever need.

"I suspect my aunt wants to remove to Bath or Brighton. She detests country life, and the way she keeps playing the invalid card makes certain she doesn't need to help around the property." She wet her bottom lip. "I suspect Uncle will break soon and give in to her wish to relocate. He's quite browbeaten already."

"And if you're not betrothed?" He hated that he hung on her every word, but he couldn't help it.

Elinor wrapped the shawl tighter about her shoulders. "I suppose I'll go with them. I cannot very well stay here and work in the bakery, can I? After all, the house is too large for one woman to ramble around in, and my pittance at the shop won't lend itself to renting a cottage, let alone feeding myself as well."

Not to mention, if she moved, there would be no more clandestine visits through the passageway—not that it had become a habit yet. This was only the second time. He shook his head to clear his wandering thoughts. It was much too early to worry. "In any event, I'm glad you're here tonight." He closed the distance between them then fingered the crocheted shawl. "I apologize, but this is the ugliest garment I've ever seen." It was stiff and rough beneath his fingertip. "It cannot possibly be comfortable."

"It's not, and it does scratch my skin, but since it was the only thing my mother made for me, I wear it occasionally."

"Did she often do handiwork?"

"Heavens no. She wasn't good at domestic tasks like knitting or crochet, but they made her happy so no one complained." She held his gaze and let the shawl slip to the floor. "Besides, I accidentally left my gray one here the other night." Her voice had developed that same smoky quality that never failed to set fire to his blood.

"Do you not own other pieces?" If he continued to look into her eyes, he'd fall in and become lost. Perhaps that wasn't such a bad idea. He ran a finger along the neckline of her dress. When she shivered, he replaced his fingers with his lips and the slope of rose-scented skin became the beginning of his undoing. His cock thickened and pressed against his trousers.

"I do, but I wanted to be sure to arrive when you finished your work, and the black shawl, for all its ugliness, is warm." She manipulated the buttons on his waistcoat since he wasn't wearing a tailcoat as he hadn't gone out of the house all day. "Did you wish to engage me in conversation tonight, Mr. Ansley, or will we be occupied with other matters?"

"Geoffrey. I asked you to call me Geoffrey." The words rasped from his throat while he shrugged out of the vest. It joined her shawl on the floor.

"Very well. What did you have planned for tonight... Geoffrey?" She tugged his shirt front from his trousers and slipped her hands beneath to rest on his chest. Heat blazed over his skin to rival the warmth coming from the fireplace. "I hope it requires making use of the bed." She looked up at him through the veil of her lashes and his knees threatened to buckle. "Or, I could pleasure you with my mouth. Since you did such a thing to me, I've been wondering what it would be like to provide you with that sort of bliss."

"Good God, you'll be my death." He pulled her into his arms and kissed her as if his life depended upon it. Her soft lips gave way to his, and she eagerly opened her mouth, inviting him in, even went so far as to entice his tongue with hers, and once he thrust inside, she gently sucked on that organ. His imaginings went wild as he replaced his tongue with his prick in his mind. His cock pulsed as if it, too, had the same idea. Eventually, he wrenched away, his breathing labored, and his body heated. "How do you know about such things?"

The grin she shot him had the power to melt his bones. "I've heard stories from working in the village and from listening to the maids. Beatrice told me a tale a year ago of how a man and woman can pleasure each other by mouth at the same time." Curiosity shadowed her eyes. "And once I saw one of the maids let the man who delivers milk and eggs put his member into her mouth while they were hidden in a dark corner of the kitchen."

Was there nothing Elinor would not surprise him with? He whipped off his shirt then tossed it away. "Let us see how the night progresses, but I assure you, there will be much pleasure."

"There will be indeed." She dropped to her knees before him. "I wish to explore you as you did me. It's only fair."

His heart tightened. "My girl, how is it possible my adoration for you grows with each time I see you?" Did she comprehend what exactly she intended to do? Even as he waited on her reply, he slid the buttons of his trousers free of their holes.

"I wouldn't know. I am merely attempting to enjoy myself and what you mean to teach me." Elinor licked her lips as she drew down the flap of his trousers and pushed aside the soft fabric of his short pants. "I never grow tired of seeing your member."

"Yet you've only seen it a few times." At least those he'd known about. If she'd been spying on him since the first, who knows what she'd seen. Geoffrey sucked in a breath the second she caressed his rigid flesh. "Go gently. Too much handling will end the night quite abruptly, and I'll be put out, for I very much wish to have relations with you." He dropped his hands to her shoulders as he widened his stance. "Slowly. It is not a race, and neither are you making fire." Though her trembling touch heated him beyond what he thought he could bear.

She smoothed her hand down his length and grinned. "How do you prefer to touch this that gives you the greatest pleasure?"

"You watched me stroke myself, twice, yes?" When she nodded, he covered her hand with his, urging her fingers to curl around his shaft. The grasp of her hand, the warmth of her fingers sent heightened sensation down his spine and tore a groan from his throat. "Easy, from tip to root then back again. Once you find a rhythm, increase the speed as well as the tightness of your grip."

"I understand."

He released her hand. She slid her curled fingers down his cock. Then, at its base, she cupped his balls, gently squeezing each one before leaving off to caress and fondle them. "You're wonderful." Her fingernails scraped the sensitive flesh.

Geoffrey couldn't speak, didn't have the brain capacity to form words as she leaned forward and touched the tip of her tongue to his cock head. When she made a sound of pleasure, he inhaled sharply and exhaled with just as much force. "For God's sake, Elinor. Don't tease."

"Isn't that the point of sexual play, to tease, to bring the subject to that molten hot edge?" She wrapped her lips around his tip then flicked her silky, heated tongue over the slit, investigating the surface.

He couldn't help but watch. Did she like how the first drops of moisture tasted? He groaned again as he imagined tasting himself on her lips during a kiss. Elinor swirled her tongue over his skin. She dipped beneath the crown, ever teasing, never relenting. Geoffrey's knees wobbled, but he locked them while burying his hands into her loose-flowing tresses. "That's it, my girl." He couldn't believe she showed a proclivity for this too.

She slid one hand up the outside of his thigh and around to caress his taut buttock while wrapping the other around the base of his shaft and moving farther down his length. Little by little she took his cock into her mouth. Geoffrey shivered at the exquisite feelings racing up his length. He fought the urge to thrust and chose instead to let her continue her exploration. She stroked his flesh with both tongue and fingers then pulled back, scraping him lightly with her teeth as she went. He cursed under his breath as his member pulsed. He'd spend soon. It was all too much. She sucked the tip, releasing it only to repeat the action with greater strength.

"Damnation, woman, I won't survive the night if you keep on." He pushed deep into her mouth, and she gagged. "I apologize for my zeal." He retreated, sliding free from her warmth. "Do you wish to continue?"

"Oh yes." Her wicked smile sent liquid heat through his veins. "It's quite an interesting prospect to pleasure a man this way." Once more she advanced on his cock, and this time she set a slow, gentle rhythm, taking him as deep as she could manage then easing off. Each time she drew back, she squeezed his girth.

"Elinor..." Geoffrey slid his hands further into her hair and curved his fingers around her skull as his thrusts grew more frantic. His heartbeat accelerated to match. "I'm losing control." His member pulsed and twitched. As he watched his shaft slide in and out of her mouth, saliva making it slick and glistening, heat swirled through his insides, and they clenched in anticipation. A strangled sound ripped from his throat. He wrenched from her mouth. Stumbling a few steps, he gasped from the exquisite ache she'd left in him. "Take off your clothes then lay on the bed." Even to his own ears, his command sounded shaky and full of angst.

She frowned. "I wanted to taste you."

A groan escaped his throat. She presented such a ravishing picture as she knelt with an expression of disappointment and passion-filled eyes that he very nearly took her right there on the floor. But he had other, sweeter plans. "I want to torment you as payment for your ministrations just now." He pulled her into a standing position, but the temptation of her red, swollen lips were too much of a distraction. Geoffrey tugged her against him and kissed her hard.

When he broke the embrace, he pushed her in the direction of the bed. "I mean it. Undress or I'll do it for you, and I cannot guarantee your dress will remain in one piece." The air on his wet cock rapidly cooled the skin.

Curiosity lit her gaze. "That sounds exciting."

"Scoot." He swatted her bottom then strode across the floor to an armoire. After opening one of the doors, he yanked out a drawer and removed two cravats. The soft cotton would provide strong bonds but not bite into her tender skin. "Once you're finished, lie on your stomach."

"Why? Don't I need to be on my back?" Her words were muffled by her dress as she struggled out of it.

"You have much to learn." Geoffrey draped the cravats around his neck then toed out of his boots. Once he'd kicked free of them, he shucked out of his trousers and short pants. His cock throbbed with need. The time sliding in and out of her mouth hadn't given much relief. "You'll enjoy this."

As would he. Already the thought of burying himself to the hilt in her heat had his member jumping.

As soon as she was in the position he'd requested, Geoffrey joined her. With her body laid out and her porcelain skin on display and the tempting curve of her arse waiting for him, she made an exquisite picture. "Good God, Elinor. You're a siren." He took one of her wrists, tied one end of a cravat around it then knotted the other end to the bed frame.

"You're binding me?" Anxiety sounded in her voice.

"Yes. It will force you to concentrate on your own pleasure." He moved around to the other side of the bed then gave the same treatment to her other hand. "Try the bonds."

When she pulled at the cravats, they gave her a bit of slack but mostly kept her immobile. Seeing her laid out thusly for *his* pleasure tightened his chest and sent urgent pulses into his cock. "Excellent. Now we'll commence."

"You won't hurt me, will you?" She glanced at him over her shoulder, her eyes wide.

"Absolutely not." Geoffrey climbed onto the bed then stroked a hand down her back. "I merely wish to infuse a little play into our tryst tonight." He maneuvered between her legs, spreading them wide. The minx wriggled her hips, which put her nether bits on display, all pink and glistening with her arousal. "Do you trust me?" The last thing he wanted was for her to fear their coming together.

"Yes." The word was fraught with trepidation. Her whole body jerked when he leaned over her and slid both hands beneath her. His cock, pressing against the crease of her arse, ached with the need for release. As best he could, Geoffrey ignored it in the quest to bring her to release. He brushed his fingers over the hard peaks of her nipples. "Oh yes, Geoffrey."

He grinned at the change in her voice. Nothing except excitement came from her now. "That's what I like to hear." Over and over, he fondled the pebbled tips. Then he left off and caressed the smooth skin of her hips. "I'm so glad I found you in my wall two days ago." The dip at the small of her back occupied his attention. He stroked his fingers over it then moved down the bed and pressed his lips to the spot. "You've brought a breath of fresh air to my homecoming."

Elinor squirmed. She pulled at her bonds. "It turned out to be the best adventure."

"An adventure, you say?" His heart squeezed. Why did he want their time together to be more permanent than a mere dalliance? He, who had wished for nothing more than to be left alone to study his law books and perhaps find acceptance in the land of his birth? *I refuse to think about that right now.* Instead, he slid a hand over the sweet curve of her buttocks then slipped it between her thighs. His fingers glided through her drenched folds. "I adore how wet you are for me." He continued on and penetrated her heat with first one finger then two.

The bedclothes muffled her response, but she wriggled her hips. With every thrust of his hand, tiny sounds of pleasure escaped her. The cravats securing her wrists pulled taut. His erection tightened. A few drops of moisture beaded on its tip. He'd spend soon. Elinor dug her knees into the mattress and pushed upward, almost into a position of supplication.

Geoffrey smiled. "Now that is an excellent idea." He removed his fingers only to grip her hips and settled himself between her splayed legs on his knees. His cock bumped her slick entrance. Just that tiny bit of stimulation sent urgent tingles through his length. Damnation it would be quick. "It seems where you're concerned, I have no finesse for the preliminaries. I cannot wait to claim your body."

"I have no complaints." She rested her cheek against the mattress. "I desperately want to feel you inside me."

"Your wish is my command, fair lady." With a flex of his hips, he pushed into her heat and didn't stop until he was fully seated. His moan mingled with hers. Her tight inner walls closed around him, hugging him. He set a quick rhythm since the angle of their joining would guarantee a fast descent into bliss.

"Mmm, yes." She rocked backward as much as her bonds would allow, meeting each thrust. "More. Harder. Let me really feel how much you adore doing this with me."

His chest clenched, not from need but from something much stronger. "I think I've corrupted you, my girl." He encouraged her further onto her knees so that her arse was clearly in the air and adjusted his strokes accordingly. Over and over, he pounded into her, watching his shaft, wet from her juices, slide in and out. "You're taking to depravity with too much relish." He loved how she put every ounce of feeling into moving with him.

"If this is what wickedness is, I should have done it earlier in my life." She gasped. "But then I wouldn't have met you." She wrapped her fingers around her bonds. "I must say, having you as a neighbor has made the sting of missing Beatrice ease."

He didn't want to be a placeholder. "Tell me you want me." Digging his fingers into her hips, he increased his pace. "Tell me you think of me for more than a neighbor." He reached one hand around and strummed her swollen, slick button. "Tell me, damn it." The passion in his tone surprised him. Never had he begged a woman for anything.

"Oh." Elinor's moan sounded very much like it had in the wall that first night he discovered her spying on him. "I want you in my bed, all the time. What we share is..." Another moan cut into her speech as he continued to torment her nub. She gasped for breath. "... beautiful, naughty, and every bit as exciting as I dreamed."

They were perfectly good words but didn't leave him feeling any better about what they were doing. He was supposed to be a gentleman, not taking advantage of her simply for the ease of the passageway that connected their homes. "I suppose that's good for now."

"For the love of God, stop talking and finish me. I'm so close." Annoyance threaded through her voice as she wriggled her hips.

Geoffrey smiled. He adored her affinity for bed sport. As he increased his thrusts, he plucked her button. Seconds later, her body stiffened, and her inner walls contracted around him. She cried out his name as she writhed in the grip of her release, and his heart skipped a beat. Too bad he couldn't see her expression in such a position. He'd wager she'd be glorious. Then hot sensation shot along his cock and tightened his balls. His orgasm roared through him, and he pushed once more through the contractions milking his length. This time, he didn't withdraw.

Finally, when his cock ceased its frantic pulsing, he collapsed against her back. His weight eased her body into the mattress, and he rested his head on her shoulder as his ragged breathing mingled with hers in the sudden quiet of the room.

"Though I enjoyed not having the use of my hands, in the future, I'd prefer being unbound, as I like be able to touch you and watch your face." She stirred beneath him, and he immediately sprang off her. "Would that be acceptable?"

"Yes, of course. I merely thought to introduce you to something new." Though she'd been a virgin when he first introduced her to carnal play, her propensity for spying and seeing him in intimate moments left him assuming she'd be more adventurous than other misses might. Perhaps he shouldn't have anticipated her willingness. Geoffrey frowned while he untied her wrists. Once they were free, he took her hands in his and drew her to the edge of the bed. "Elinor, it would seem my conscience cannot let me continue unless I ask for your hand." He owed her much more than using her as a bed partner merely for the convenience.

"I beg your pardon?" She yanked away while her eyes went wide, and distrust clouded their depths.

"Marry me. I've comprised you beyond all reason." He raked a hand through his hair, knowing he must sound like a loon. "You'll still have your freedom, but you'll enjoy my protection. At least then people won't talk."

"You think a hasty wedding will prevent rumors?" Her chuckle was a bitter affair. "More likely it will cause them all the more." She struggled from the bed then stood before him, flushed and naked, and in a full-blown case of outrage.

"Well, I thought it the honorable thing to do." Why couldn't she understand he was trying to protect her? "At least this way, you and I can continue to enjoy each other without risk of being found out. It's only a matter of time."

She planted her hands on her hips. "You don't love me. Isn't that what marriage should be based on?"

"Well, I..." How to explain how he felt when he wasn't certain himself? "All I know is that I feel something more substantial than lust for you. Wouldn't you rather give it a chance to grow into something more?"

"No." With a frown, she scurried across the room and plucked her shift from the pile of clothes on the floor. As she smoothed it over her body, she said, "Long ago I made the decision to never marry. No matter that I enjoy what you and I share, I cannot go back on that promise."

"Why?" He left the bed and closed the distance between them. "Let me do this for you. At least you'll always be taken care of no matter what happens with your uncle." The protection he'd felt since meeting her tripled. If any woman needed a man to look after her and support her, it was Elinor.

"I'm sorry." She shook her head then retrieved her dress and put it on. "I refuse to open myself up to more hurt if you should die, or God forbid, what if we should have children and for some reason, disaster befalls them?" Tears shimmered in her dark eyes. "I couldn't bear that. Not after losing my family."

"You don't know what the future holds. Just because you've had misfortune before does not mean you'll continue to do so." He reached for her, but she danced away. "Elinor, please." When she merely shook her head again, he sighed. "So, to your way of thinking, if you and I don't marry, my untimely death will be easier to swallow? Would you feel less if we weren't man and wife?"

"That is beside the point." Her expression was unreadable.

"No, it's not." Geoffrey grabbed her hand. "You've already said you trust me. Well, I'm in earnest again now. If we marry, if will help the both of us, and we'll have enjoyment besides." The more he thought about the impromptu plan, the more he warmed to it. No longer did he wish to find a mistress. He wanted his fiery redheaded neighbor, and above all, he wanted to spend the rest of his existence making her happy. She'd had a less than ideal experience with life up until now. At the very least, he could show her the next twenty-seven years could be wonderful. "If you won't agree now, will you promise me you'll think about it?"

"I suppose, but I must warn you, my answer will be the same regardless of how much time passes." She tugged her hand from his, scooped up her slippers and shawl then headed to the hidden panel. When she glanced at him from over her shoulder, a tear had fallen to her cheek. "I truly am sorry I couldn't agree to your suit."

"Think nothing of it, my girl." He yanked a dressing gown from its place draped on a chair. Once he'd wrapped the garment around himself and pulled the sash, he gave her a bright smile that didn't reflect his feelings. "Be warned. I intend to call on you tomorrow. And the day after that, and every day following until you see my logic."

In the space of a few heartbeats, she'd opened the panel and slipped into the darkened passageway beyond.

Geoffrey stared after her then chuckled as he slid the panel closed. For the first time since arriving in Surrey, he had a clear goal: winning Elinor's hand, if only to save her from herself, but beyond that, the woman had wormed her way into his heart simply by being herself. That alone warranted more investigation.

You can run, my adorable ghost in the wall, but eventually you won't be able to ignore the state of your heart.

Chapter Eight

Elinor's stomach knotted with nerves as she sat next to Geoffrey on the settee in the parlor. True to his word, he'd come to call for tea; only this time, he'd spoken to her uncle before she was ever informed he'd arrived. Now, her uncle beamed at her from the other settee while Nigel, the horrid brat, hoarded scones as if they'd suddenly become scarce.

"I never thought you'd make a match, Elinor, but I'm pleased Mr. Ansley came up to scratch," her uncle mentioned as he broke of a piece of sugar from the loaf and dropped it into his teacup. "I told him that of course I'd give my permission. Now I can stop pushing you at Baron Underhill's sons."

"While that is a relief, I fail to see how a marriage between Geoffrey and I will be beneficial for either of us." She clutched her teacup in both hands to still their shaking. It was outside of enough that he proposed directly following their session the night before, but to involve her uncle in securing her promise? They could both go to the devil.

"Of course it will benefit you." Her uncle frowned. "He's shown himself to be a right proper man who'll be an asset to Surrey."

Tired of trying to keep the tea from sloshing out of her cup, she leaned forward and set it on the table, conscious the whole time of Geoffrey's presence beside her. The heat from his body seeped into hers, which recalled her to what she'd done to him last night and how he'd taken her after that. Warmth flooded her cheeks. Never in all her wildest fantasies had she thought she'd have intimate relations in such a fashion, but there had been something about it... A delicious tingle slid down her spine and lodged between her thighs.

When he'd driven into her hard and fast, and she had no recourse except to receive him and concentrate on her own pleasure, she'd felt... free and desired. In her whole life, no one of her acquaintance had actually needed her. Now that her relationship with Geoffrey had accelerated into one of carnality, she supposed he needed her. Granted, this was only for physical fulfillment, but it was a start. As she sat back, Elinor avoided his gaze; for once she looked at him, she'd be swamped by emotions she didn't want nor know how to handle.

Uncle slurped his tea. "And it couldn't come at a better time, I can tell you."

"Why?" She glanced at him, her frown deepening.

Geoffrey leaned close, put his lips to her ear and whispered, "I much prefer it when you smile. You're beautiful when you do."

Heat singed her insides. Her heartbeat skittered. He was the only man of her acquaintance to tell her that, multiple times. She slid her gaze to his and her stomach fluttered at the sincerity in his expression. "Thank you." The answering whisper forced past her tight throat. What was he about?

Her uncle clapped his hands, which bounced her attention back to him. "I'm taking your aunt and Nigel to Brighton for a few weeks during the winter holidays. One of your aunt's relatives is getting married and she wants to help with preparations."

Nigel sprang from his chair. Scone crumbs fell from his clothing like snowflakes. "I don't want to go to smelly old Brighton. It stinks of fish there, and I hate the sea. I want to spend Christmas here, not at some crumbling pile with moldy old relatives."

"You're going," her uncle said with stern warning in his voice. "Run along, Nigel. I'm sure you're bored."

"I'm always bored when you talk about Ellie. She's a mess, and now that she's got this git in her pocket, she'll put on airs, just like I said she would." He glared at Geoffrey. "You're as mad as she is." He stole a lump of sugar from the tray then ran out of the room.

"At least I have fine company in my madness." Geoffrey cleared his throat. "Mr. Adelaide, perhaps you could give Elinor and I a moment to talk? I'm afraid all of this has come as quite a shock to her, and me as well."

"This is true," Elinor interjected. "I was rather shocked." And somewhat flattered when he'd asked her the night before. However, she'd also meant what she'd told him. She didn't intend to marry anyone. Her heart wasn't strong enough to survive another death of one close to her. She kept her gaze on the toes of her slippers. What she couldn't understand was how quickly she'd come to regard Geoffrey as someone whom she could conceivably care for if she'd let herself.

"Very well, but the parlor door will remain open, and I'll just be across the hall in the library should you have need of me.

At least we can observe the proprieties until you're wed." Her uncle stood, as did Geoffrey.

Elinor stifled an unladylike snort. What would he say if he knew she'd snuck through the secret passageway and had not only spied upon Geoffrey naked but had also been bedded by him—twice—let him pleasure her with his mouth and had done the same to him? The heat in her cheeks intensified. It would seem since meeting him, she'd become quite the wanton, and with no remorse. "Thank you."

"You're lucky, Ellie. Mr. Ansley intends to marry you as soon as the banns are read. You'll have a life many in the village will envy. He'll provide well for you."

"I never wanted that sort of life. I merely wish to..." To what? Before Geoffrey moved to Surrey and she began spying on him, she wanted only to forget that she was nearly alone in the world. There was also the fear of being with someone who merely tolerated the kind of woman she was instead of embracing all of her. But now? Did she want something more? Slowly, she raised her gaze to Geoffrey's. The humor sparkling in his green eyes warmed her insides. "Right now, I need to discuss the situation further."

"You'll have fifteen minutes. Don't want all the mysteries between you solved before that big day. There's something about the not knowing that spurs a man forward." Her uncle patted her on the top of her head as he would a dog on his way out.

Once alone with Geoffrey, Elinor's nerves got the best of her. She darted away from him, coming to pause near one of the windows. "I haven't changed my mind." Outside, rain and gray skies dampened the world, a fitting tribute to the scattered state of her mind.

"Neither have I." His baritone voice sounded directly behind her. "I still believe we would be a good fit."

She spun and faced him. "Why? You know nothing about me except rumors and gossip."

"I know a bit more than that, wouldn't you say?" He advanced a step, and when she retreated, her backside hit the windowsill.

"Oh, do you mean because of our...?" Elinor fluttered a hand between them. "...our being intimate?"

When he grinned, a wicked glint appeared in his eyes. "Among other things." Geoffrey took one of her hands. "You've shared the story of your past with me, and I know you have a tender, caring heart even though you try so hard to keep it locked away to prevent hurting."

"But you don't know my secrets."

He raised an eyebrow. "I know the big one, the one that prompts you to bring yourself to pleasure with your fingers." He dropped his voice. "And sneak about my walls, spying on me when I do the same, both of which make my blood burn to whisk you away and do naughty things to you."

Moisture trickled between her thighs. Need throbbed deep inside her. His idea sounded like heaven. Elinor shook her head. She had to remain strong. "None of that explains why you wish to marry me. You have to admit, I'm not the best catch in Guildford. You could find release with any woman."

"I could, but I chose to do so with you."

She frowned as he held her gaze. Every time she peered deep into his eyes, she had the strangest sensation of falling from a vast height, but she was never afraid. At the back of her mind, she trusted him to catch her. "Surely there are others you're interested in and can align your name with to further your position."

"Perhaps, for me, it's not about position and rank." He squeezed her fingers. "For all of my mother's silly ways, she did find the love of her life, and for a while, she was happy. Finding love and sharing it soothes the ills of everything else in life."

Her heart skipped a beat. Did that mean he loved her?

"Elinor." He tugged her closer until she had no choice but to rest her free hand on his chest. "Is it outside the realm of possibility I'd like to be happy in life and would like to make you happy too? I suspect you've had precious little to make you smile in recent years. Why not let me take on the challenge?"

"I don't suppose it is, but I am having trouble understanding why me?" She tried to pull her hand from his. He tightened his grip. "If you are only doing this because you feel you've ruined me or compromised me, I can assure you, that isn't true and won't have any bearing on my future. No one wanted me before you came along." Her chest ached at hearing her prospects put so bluntly.

"True, one of the reasons I asked is to protect your name and reputation, but then, I cannot escape my manners." His grin softened and the look in his eye put her in mind of a man bent on romance. "If we took all of that away, forgot about niceties and Society and conventions, you still fascinate me at every level, and I want to know everything about you. It's more than most marriages have to build upon."

"But your clients and business connections—"

"Cannot be any more adversely affected or put into shadow. People will either choose to trust me or they won't." He lifted her hand to his lips then placed a kiss upon its back. "If we throw all your objections onto the proverbial bonfire with everything else, I'm just a man trying to become a solicitor who'd like to do that with a crazy, red-haired wife by his side."

A tremble moved down her spine. Would she fit into his life, and what was more, did she want to? And what would happen if something happened to him or he left? "It's folly to do this." She didn't know if she wanted to convince him or herself.

"You think that now because you weigh every decision you make against the horrible things that have already occurred, but what's life without a gamble every now and then?"

"So, wedding me will be a gamble?" Elinor was stuck between the window and the immovable wall of his chest, but his body heat seeped into her and left a delicious throb between her thighs. For one insane moment, she considered giving in to his request. What would it be like to have a man willingly take care of her, pledge his heart to her for the rest of his life?

"The sweetest kind." His eyes darkened just like they had right before when he'd tied her to his bed. Goose flesh broke out over her skin. "Since I'm throwing a rout in a few days, which just happens to be on Guy Fawke's night, would you feel more comfortable in giving me your answer then? I've had my new butler, Carmichael, issue invites to the area gentry but also to many of the villagers. There should be a decent mix." When he smiled, the skin at the corners of his eyes crinkled and gave him an air of approachability. "Your uncle said it would be the perfect event in which to announce the engagement. I'd like to publicly tell the world you are mine."

His. Belonging to someone. She shook her head even as she wanted to melt against him. "I've already told you I won't change my mind. I won't marry anyone. It's too great a risk."

Geoffrey dipped his head toward hers, so close that their lips nearly met. His breath warmed her cheek. "Anything good and wonderful in life is worth the risk. How else are we to know its value?" He brushed his lips against hers. "Let me take care of you, Elinor, and help carry your fears as well as vanquish them. I want to be the man who'll always rescue you."

"Mmm, I..." Her tongue felt glued to the roof of her mouth. His actions were too much and overwhelmed her.

He caressed her cheek. "For once, live with abandon and let yourself chase happiness. I promise it will be good for you."

When she would have slipped her arms around his neck and encouraged him to give her a proper kiss, he pulled away and retreated a few steps, leaving her with a racing heart and stumbling to keep her footing. "Oh." She ran the tip of her tongue along her bottom lip. "Yes. I'll give you my answer then." A restless feeling settled over her. She dropped her voice. "Should I, ah, visit you tonight?"

"That won't be necessary," he answered in a matching whisper. Geoffrey winked. "Until the matter of our engagement is settled, I'd rather not have physical temptation forcing your hand. I want you to accept me based solely on the quiet murmurs of your heart." As her uncle appeared in the doorway, Geoffrey cleared his throat. "Well then, Miss Bennett, I shall see you at my party or rout or whatever they choose to call it. I look forward to hearing what you have to say."

Elinor stared into the empty room long after the men had departed. Geoffrey was a clever one, all right. A smile tugged at her lips. She didn't need him for sexual release, though she had to admit, such a thing did feel better when his arms were around her and his body was pressed against hers.

November 5th

Elinor frowned. Across the drawing room, Geoffrey laughed and talked with a pretty woman with black, curly hair. Despite the butterflies in her belly from wearing a new gown of green silk overlaid with silver lace, threads of jealousy spiked her chest. Why was he conversing with another woman when he should be waiting for her to answer his question? Well, if he thought he could play the rogue without recourse, he'd be wrong. She smoothed her hands down the front of her skirt then wound through the crush of people until she reached the two of them.

"Good evening, Mr. Ansley. I've had the devil's own time locating you tonight." She hardly blinked an eye at the lie or the vulgar language. The situation warranted it, and besides, her aunt and uncle were occupied in talking to a man whose blond hair was caught back with a leather tie.

Geoffrey's expression held surprise. Was he interested in courting the other woman? "I'm so glad you're here, Miss

Bennett." As he grinned, his eyes twinkled, darkening to emerald, and her heart squeezed. That look meant mischief.

"Are you?" She couldn't help the terse tone of her voice. "It seems to me you've forgotten all about me. You've been hither and yon conversing with nearly everyone."

The twinkle turned into a knowing glint. "Of course. No cause to be jealous." He drew an arm around her waist. "Margaret Cavendish, this is my bride-to-be, Elinor Bennett."

Warmth spread through Elinor at the announcement as well as his show of ownership, but then the pleasure turned to simmering anger at his high-handedness at telling anyone before she'd agreed. "Actually, I'm still considering Mr. Ansley's offer."

A slight expression of disappointment appeared on Margaret's face. Then she recovered with an ecstatic smile. "How wonderful for you both." The woman's brown eyes reflected nothing but joy. "When can we expect the announcement?"

"Tonight, if I can persuade her," Geoffrey said with another grin. "She can be quite stubborn."

Elinor shivered as he rubbed his thumb at her waist. Answering tremors erupted in her core. She'd missed visiting him the last couple of nights. "No more stubborn than you." She glanced between them. "How do you know each other?"

"Oh, Geoffrey and my brother, James, were old school chums. We've only now become reacquainted." Margaret's smile was warm. "I wasn't certain James would let me come tonight, but in the end, he decided to give Geoffrey a chance despite the rumors."

"I see." Elinor's stomach twinged. Old acquaintances. Margaret was more suited to be Geoffrey's bride. They had history. She peered into Geoffrey's face, and the pride beaming from his expression tightened her chest. "If you will excuse me? I'd like to talk to someone who has just arrived." Without waiting for permission, she put as much distance, and as many people, as she could between them. *I need to think.* And she couldn't do that being so close to him.

She ducked behind a grouping of potted ferns and collapsed into one of the chairs arranged in a pleasing collection. Her pulse hammered, swished in her ears. Elinor rubbed her fingers over her heart. *How silly, a heart truly aching, and over a man no less.* Yet it was true. And all because that other woman would be a better match for Geoffrey than she would. *Nonsense, Ellie. Stop it.* Geoffrey merely knew the other woman longer. That was all. Would this how life would be then? Her always questioning motives?

"Excuse me. Do you mind if I sit here with you? I'm exhausted and have no idea when my husband will be finished with his visiting."

Elinor left off contemplating the ferns and whipped around in her seat. A woman stood before her, her black hair in ringlets that framed her face and her blue eyes wide and shadowed with fatigue. "Of course."

"Thank you." Once the newcomer had seated herself and arranged her rose-colored silk skirts, she sighed. "I don't enjoy parties now that I'm *enceinte*," she confided. "Not that I did before. I'd much prefer to be back in the Lake District with Collin."

Elinor's mind spun. "I'm sorry but do we know each other?" She couldn't understand why a stranger would reveal such intimate details of their life.

"Oh, probably not." The other woman smiled. "I forget things so easily now. I'm Vicountess Blackpool, Vanessa Northington, formerly Underhill. At times I can scarcely believe I was married just three months ago."

"Actually, now that you've mentioned it, I vaguely remember the stories about your runaway bride days." Elinor gave the woman another look. "Pardon me, but you don't appear with child." Except for a slightly rounded stomach and pale cheeks, Vanessa seemed the picture of glowing health.

"How kind of you to say." She smoothed a hand over her belly. "I can't wait to be a mother, and to see if the babe will resemble me or Collin."

She sounded so thrilled and so earnest that a tiny stab of jealousy moved through Elinor. "Are you visiting your family? I haven't yet seen your parents tonight."

A delicate laugh escaped Vanessa. "Oh, you wouldn't. Mama made me a promise on my wedding day to stop shoving her nose into other people's business around the county. I threatened to never visit unless she abided by it." She flashed another serene smile. "In any event, since I'm in Surrey, I wanted the diversion of an entertainment, and to get a look at Mr. Ansley, before I'm too busy."

"Get a look at him? Why?"

"Why not? He's easy on the eyes, I'll give you that. And gossip surrounds him, which means he must be a good sort." She arched an eyebrow. "A person steeped in rumor is always the best to chum around with."

"You might be right." Elinor chewed on her bottom lip. "Have you told your parents about your good news?"

"Tomorrow's the day. I know it's early yet, but I'm so excited I might burst. Papa will be beside himself."

"How about your brothers?" At the last second, Elinor stifled a shudder.

"They won't care. Honestly, I don't think they've accepted Collin as my husband yet." A shrug lifted Vanessa's shoulders. "They're not perfect, but they're my family."

"Where is your husband?" Curiosity circled through her head. Her companion had married a viscount after a scandalous story of how her husband had kidnapped her while in the guise of a highwayman.

Vanessa craned her neck then said, "Just there. The dashing blond man in black."

Elinor sucked in a breath as the man in question—the same one talking with her aunt and uncle—turned slightly as he nodded at something her uncle said. The left side of his face was puckered and scarred. "Oh my."

"Isn't he handsome?" Vanessa clutched Elinor's hand. "I cannot believe he's mine. I wake up feeling incredibly lucky. I love him so much." The last was said on a breathy sigh.

For the first time Elinor understood how wonderful opening up to another person could be. The enamored expression on Vanessa's face caused tears to crowd her throat. "You don't worry about losing him to the calamity of life?"

"No, why should I?" The other woman frowned. "I cannot control what happens in the future. My husband survived a horrible war halfway across the world and believes in living life to the fullest. I do, as well. For now, I have Collin in my life. I refuse to worry away my time with him by wondering over what might happen. Why mar the time he and I have together?"

"I wish I could adopt your outlook." She cast her gaze around the crowded room and finally spotted Geoffrey. He still conversed with Margaret, and to her way of thinking, was standing entirely too close to her.

"I've heard whispers that Mr. Ansley offered for you," Vanessa interjected. "Have you accepted?"

Elinor sighed. She transferred her attention to her new friend—or, at least the woman she hoped would be a friend if she'd allow herself to trust again. Could she open herself to more people beyond Geoffrey and perhaps make friends and take chances? "Not yet. I'm conflicted. Look at him! How can he be serious about marrying me when he's flirting with another woman?"

"He's merely talking to her." Vanessa rolled her eyes. "He's not touching her or trying to brush against her. Don't take everything personally. That will kill your romance before it ever has a chance to grow."

Am I doing exactly that? Her heart still vaguely ached. If she was at sixes and sevens now by watching him interact with a woman, how would she feel if she gave into the urge to care for him and something happened to him?

Vanessa touched her hand. "I know from experience. Collin and I had a few personal misunderstandings before we decided to trust each other."

"I do trust Geoffrey..." How to explain when her reasoning made her seem silly or naïve?

"Only you can make that decision, of course, but I will say marriage to a wonderful man is quite something every woman should experience."

"It's too soon." How could he even know the state of his heart when she couldn't figure out hers?

A giggle escaped the other woman's throat. "I had the same argument, but Collin convinced me that the length of time two people know each other before love blooms is irrelevant. It... happens." Vanessa rose. "That being said, your future husband is coming this way, and I need to claim mine."

"Oh, well, it's been lovely to meet you." Even if Elinor had wished Vanessa would be a friend, how could it happen if the woman left Surrey so soon? "I had hoped we could visit further."

"Absolutely we can. I'll be in Surrey for a few weeks yet. Please say you'll stop by my parents' home. We'll talk more when there's more time." She sucked in a sudden breath. "I'm feeling rather indisposed and would rather not cast up my accounts into a plant."

Geoffrey arrived shortly after Vanessa departed and held out a hand to Elinor. "Would you do me the honor of a dance?" With him looking so devastating in his dark evening clothes and with the lock of hair threatening to tumble over his forehead, how could she refuse?

She slipped her hand in his and allowed him to pull her to her feet. "Actually, I would much rather go somewhere private."

"Oh?" So much hope rested in that one, tiny word that Elinor regretted what she was about to do.

"I need to talk to you." Her stomach cramped. Tears crowded her throat. The trouble with allowing herself to feel more than temporal things for anyone was that when her heart became engaged, it hurt all the more if things went wrong. She pressed a hand to her heart while Geoffrey led her through the room then out onto a terrace similar to the one where she first kissed him. She hated that she'd need to hurt him, but if they parted on the heels of an argument, it wouldn't hurt as much as losing him to fate.

The chilly air skated across her heated skin. Goose flesh rippled along her arms and tightened her nipples. She crossed her arms over her breasts. "I should jump right to it."

"You should, especially if I'm to be made the happiest of men." He wrapped his arms around her, twirling them around in an impromptu dance before holding her in a loose embrace. "Well?"

She looked past his shoulder to all of the lanterns that illuminated the terrace. Later in the evening, closer to midnight, Geoffrey would burn a bonfire and they'd all celebrate with toasts and hot cider. In other circumstances, it could have been a lovely, romantic scene. "I cannot marry you." She despised that her voice shook.

"You'll have to provide me a more valid reason than the ones you've already given." When he dipped his head to kiss her, she reared back. "Elinor, what's wrong?" Concern rang in his voice.

The heat from his body tempted her. It was all too inviting, reminding her he'd be a solid presence in her life, the man she could always count on to be there with support and understanding if she needed it. A tremble shot down her spine. She would wound him terribly, but he wouldn't listen to her reasoning. The man wouldn't accept her previous excuses.

Perhaps he was besotted enough to ignore what would only be hurdles they'd both had to jump, so she needed to find something that would resonate with him, hurt him irrevocably. Her stomach clenched. "Dear heavens, this won't be easy." She worried her bottom lip, took a deep breath then finally blurted out, "I could never wed a bastard. Maybe you should go back to New York where you're wanted. Surrey has a certain standard of conduct, and you won't ever aspire to it."

Shock jumped into his eyes. "What's gotten into you?" He relaxed his grip, and she scampered backward. "You don't mean that."

"Oh, but I do." Her words sounded all too croaky. Unshed tears burned her eyes. "I was perfectly content to leave our relationship at the physical, but you kept on. It isn't your place to worry about my reputation or anything else about me."

"I don't worry. I know that I want to be with you for the rest of my life." He frowned. "You said before you didn't care about my history. Now you've suddenly changed your mind? I find that highly suspect."

"Perhaps I lied." Her chest heaved from her effort to hold back the sobs that wanted to break forth. "I took what I needed from you, and now you and I are done. Goodnight, Mr. Ansley. Please don't seek me out again."

"Elinor, wait." Geoffrey closed the distance and grabbed her wrist. "What the hell is wrong? You seemed quite receptive to my suit before. Why the change?" He pulled her close. "Talk to me, my girl. We'll iron out whatever demons you believe stand in our way, and if we cannot, I vow to slay them for you."

Why did he have to be so agreeable and honorable and brave? A tear broke free and fell to her cheek. Again, he used fairy-tale language to explain her way of thinking, and she adored it. But she wrenched from his hold. "Let me go, Geoffrey. I cannot come apart with grief again. If I say yes to you that could very well happen. I cannot survive it." Her chest ached from the need to give into the wealth of tears held captive. Then Elinor ran across the terrace and raced down the stone steps. She kept running across the lawn in the direction of the fields separating his property from hers.

Devil take emotions, and commitments, and falling in love. Pushing him away hurt ten times worse than when she'd lost her family. She stumbled, fell to her knees. In that one moment, with the cold seeping into her limbs and the night closing in around her and her chest heaving with loss, clarity hit her. Perhaps it would be the wiser choice to risk fate rather than suffer such crushing pain. Then she shook her head and rose to her feet.

After everything, it would be a chance and one she didn't know if she could take. Life was too cruel for words at times.

Chapter Nine

Damn and blast. The woman was a human powder keg, and though he'd wager she hadn't meant any of the words she'd just hurled at him, he didn't know how to fix the problem. Still, his chest tightened with every breath he drew and he kept his gaze on her retreating figure until the darkness swallowed her. "Elinor!" When he would have jumped the low stone wall around the terrace and followed her, a firm grip on his shoulder prevented the action.

"Let her go." The warning, in a determined masculine voice, sounded nearby.

Geoffrey whirled around, breaking contact. "James? What the devil are you doing out here?" He stared at his childhood friend. Even after the harsh words James had delivered the other day, he'd come out to the rout. Yes, Geoffrey had talked with Margaret earlier, but he hadn't seen her brother.

"Margaret instructed me to find you and make my apologies straightaway." He clasped his hands behind his back. "Which I'm doing now. I hope you can forgive me. What I said was beneath reproach. I should have defended you." The man bowed his head, and the chilly breeze ruffled his black curls. "I was an arse."

"There's nothing to forgive, but yes, you *were* an arse. I'm glad you recognized the fact." James snorted. Geoffrey glanced again out into the night. No trace of Elinor remained, not even a flash of her gown in the faint moonlight. "Why should I not go after her?" He frowned. "I could have reached her by now and at least brought her back."

"For what purpose? She'd run again the first chance she got, and you can't very well lock her up until the party has ended. You finally are making headway in being accepted in Surrey. Are you willing to toss all of that away for a woman?"

"I would for Elinor." Geoffrey narrowed his eyes. Shock speared him as he realized it was true. There were many places in the world to live, but only one Elinor. "How do you know she'd run away from me if I pursued her tonight?" If he could ply her with kisses, he was fairly certain he could at least calm her down enough to talk.

"Women like Miss Bennett are extremely headstrong. If cornered, they will fight with all their energy until they can run again."

"She's alone in the night, James. Her temper aside, she needs my protection. It's Guy Fawkes besides, prime opportunity for mischief makers."

"There has never been an issue on this night any other year. Don't borrow trouble."

"Perhaps you're right." Geoffrey gritted his teeth against the chill in the air. He hoped Elinor had made it home.

"Your urge to play hero aside, your neighbor will be fine. While we've been talking, she's no doubt reached her home and is even now safe and sound tucked into her bed. The distance between your homes is short." James pinned him with a look brimming with compassion in the lantern light. "If she loves you like you suspect, she'll come around. Probably, she needs to convince herself or discover how she feels on her own."

Geoffrey crossed his arms over his chest. What his friend said was true. Since their homes were relatively close and Elinor had left his property at a run, she would have covered the half mile in good time. He could just imagine her huddled beneath her bedclothes. Was she crying? Did she regret what she'd said? "Why do you think I suspect she loves me?"

"You cannot help wanting a happy ending." James drew closer and looked out across the darkened lawn. "Do you remember the time when you 'suspected' Elizabeth Ellison was sweet on you?"

"We were nine. What did I know of love back then?" Yet, a smile tugged at the corners of his mouth. "I kept on though. Every day for seven days I brought her wildflowers. On that last day I gave her little mince pies and she kissed my cheek. Therefore, my suspicion was correct." As with Elinor, Elizabeth had been afraid, but she'd had that certain look in her eye, that desperation to be loved. He'd been patient and eventually she'd trusted him.

James shook his head. "You always seem to find women who are in need, and shockingly, you know exactly what to say in order to make them happy."

"Except with Elinor. If I had, she would still be here tonight, accepting my proposal." He had to do something. "I'd never forgive myself if something happened to her and I let her go." She'd looked so fetching tonight in that green gown that set off her eyes perfectly. With her fiery hair upswept and her slender, pale neck on display, she'd been the most beautiful woman in the room.

A chuckle escaped James, so unexpected, yet the sound was comforting, rife with masculine camaraderie. "You haven't changed, you know. Just like that time with Elizabeth, you have that spark in your eye. You're tip over tail for this girl."

Was he? At first, he'd thought his interest was merely a product of his manners and the need to protect her, but then, after he'd found her in his wall and had bedded her, his feelings had changed into something much deeper. A slow smile spread over his face. "I suppose I am." He, who'd come to Surrey with a mind to find a mistress, sell the house or bury himself in work. Instead, he'd met the most enchanting creature and couldn't imagine life without her on his arm, by his side, and in his bed until they both grew old.

"Good luck." James clapped him on the shoulder. "Out of all the men I know, you're vastly more suited for leg-shackling than any of them."

If only Elinor weren't so blasted stubborn. "What would you do?"

"About courtship or your current situation?"

"The current dilemma." He had no doubt his courtship would eventually prevail. After all, he knew her naughty secret. The thought of tormenting her with his fingers on her sex widened his grin. He'd do it until she said yes.

"Ask Adelaide to go back and check on her. After all, he's the girl's uncle." James turned and moved toward the door. "Barring that, once you figure it out and if you need assistance, let me know. It's the least I can do to make up for the snub."

"Thank you. I appreciate that." Geoffrey followed his friend inside. "I'll ask her uncle. Then after the party concludes, I'll check on her personally." And damn if he wouldn't ask her to marry him again. He wouldn't leave her side until she accepted.

In the end, Geoffrey sent his guests home shortly after midnight without lighting the bonfire or even serving dinner. As worried as he was for Elinor's well-being, he couldn't enjoy the conversations or anything else. He'd assembled his guests in the foyer and announced the conclusion of the rout. When a few shocked murmurs circulated, he'd gone for full disclosure and mentioned his concern for his soon-to-be bride. The company had departed in remarkably high spirits, apparently deciding his heart was in the right place. Perhaps the decision to show a bit of vulnerability would gain him clients in the future, but if it didn't, he didn't care.

Her uncle had immediately taken his wife and had departed for home, agreeing with Geoffrey's concern. They hadn't returned, so he assumed everything had been found safe and sound.

Now, as he headed toward the stairs, his mind wouldn't quiet, and all because of one red-haired woman he couldn't forget.

"Pardon me, sir." Carmichael, his recently hired butler and valet, cleared his throat.

"Yes?" Geoffrey turned. The tall, thin man, who slicked his dark hair back with pomade, his dark suit styled with military lines, stood with his back ramrod straight but an expression of high concern on his angular face. "Spit it out, man. Obviously, something is on your mind."

"Apparently Cook and some of the maids have opted to stay the night here." His tone of voice inferred this just simply wasn't done.

Geoffrey bit down on a grin. "Is there a particular reason why?"

"Cook claims 'the Guys', meaning Guy Fawkes rioters who have chosen now to organize themselves in this county, will chase them and do, and these are her exact words, sir, 'wicked, horrible things' to her and the girls if they're caught wandering through the village."

"Rioters? As far as I know, that's never happened around these parts before, has it?"

"No, Mr. Ansley. I've lived near Guildford all my life with the exception of fighting in the wars. This night is usually peaceful—unless one has issue with Catholics." His jaw worked as if he wished to say more but wasn't certain he should.

"Carmichael, if you know something else, I demand you tell me." Geoffrey's gut clenched. "Has something happened?"

"It's difficult to say since neither Cook, nor the kitchen staff, has any proof."

"Very well. Keep vigilant, as will I." Geoffrey turned and climbed the first couple of stairs. "And Carmichael, inform Cook that she and the servants are welcome to feast upon dinner as they see fit. I don't want their hard work wasted."

Carmichael nodded. "I will."

"Very good. Also, I won't require your help undressing this evening as I don't plan to go to bed until dawn in case..."

"I understand, sir." His tone conveyed perfect empathy, which was one of the reasons that Geoffrey had employed him. "Shall I have a horse saddled and at the ready?"

"No. If I need to leave, there are much quicker and stealthier ways of travel." He continued the climb to the second level then followed the corridor to his suite. Once inside his bedroom, he loosened his cravat and cursed the night in general and troublemakers in particular.

It wasn't the end to the evening he'd wanted. If all had gone well, he would have made arrangements for either Elinor to use the passageway to slip into his room or he to access hers, but now, he had no idea what would occur. His bed seemed empty without her naked body lying within the twisted sheets.

He moved to the window and looked out into the night. He hadn't lit a lantern, so no other illumination obstructed his view. "What the hell is that?" In the distance, in the direction of Elinor's home, an orange glow flickered against the dark sky. Was that fire? His stomach dropped. Was her house aflame or was it area bonfires? Even as that thought entered his head, he dismissed it. Hers was the only house in that direction. Why would her family start a bonfire for just for the few of them? Was she and her family safe? He pressed his palms to the cold glass, but didn't gain any other answers.

"Carmichael!" *Damn it all, I should have gone after her the minute she fled.* "Carmichael, get in here!"

Seconds later, his valet burst into the room, the tails of his coat streaming behind him. "Is there a problem, Mr. Ansley?"

"Of course there's a problem. Why else would I be yelling in the middle of the night?" Geoffrey raked a hand through his hair. "Come with me. We're going across to Adelaide's property. I suspect Cook was right."

Carmichael cocked a dark eyebrow. "Shall I bring a pistol, sir?"

"That would be most appreciated. Two pistols are better than none, and infinitely superior to pitchforks and torches."

Geoffrey banged a shoulder on a clump of earth inside the tunnel. "Damnation. How does she travel through here on a regular basis?" He and Carmichael had long since left the passageway from inside his house. Though that had been crowded enough for his form and his valet's to pass through, it was infinitely better than this rough-hewn tunnel of earth and stone. It stank of dirt and damp, and in some places tree roots trickled down. In others, rats skittered before the light of their swinging lanterns.

"I can only assume you're referring to Miss Bennett." Carmichael's voice sounded eerie from behind him.

"Yes. I discovered she'd been using the passageways to spy on me and my household."

"Then, if I may offer my opinion, sir. You should marry her and put an end to her nefarious activities."

A chuckle escaped Geoffrey's tight throat. "Trust me, I'm working on it."

Eventually, their trek ended at a wooden door he assumed would open into Elinor's home. "Be prepared for screaming and outraged indignation if nothing untoward has occurred here, Carmichael. We could be in a bit of a sticky wicket." The door was old and scarred wood, but had a latch. It squeaked horribly when he pulled it open.

"I'm prepared."

Geoffrey stepped into the darkness beyond and onto a landing of sorts. As he'd discovered in his house, there was a hidden panel as well as a set of narrow wooden stairs. Another cobweb-decorated passage ran toward the back of the house. "This should open into her parlor." He fumbled with the hidden spring, but once he'd located it and pressed it, the panel swung open in short order.

His assessment was correct, and he and Carmichael entered a darkened parlor without incident, but Geoffrey's heart sank upon seeing the orange glow of a fire outside the broken windows. "Vandals?"

"I wouldn't know, sir, until I have more information." Carmichael pulled his pistol from his waistband. "I'll reconnoiter the upper level."

"Excellent idea. We'll meet on the front lawn. If you find Miss Bennett or her family or their servants, shout." *And please God that they are all unharmed.*

"Very good."

As the valet bounded up the stairs, the golden light from his lantern bouncing off the walls, Geoffrey began to work the lower level. Every room he visited had broken windows. Some rooms had been violated with items thrown about and upholstery torn as if a giant had raged within. Room after room had been ransacked. In a small pantry, he came upon Mr. Adelaide and his wife, both bound and gagged, tied together back-to-back on the floor.

"Good God." Geoffrey set his lantern on a work table then spent considerable time unknotting the ropes. When he'd released the last of the bonds and they'd untied the gags, he asked, "Who did this?"

Mr. Adelaide shook his head. "There was a group of them, all masked. I don't know." He stood on shaky legs. "Where is Nigel? Elinor?"

"She's not here?" Geoffrey's pulse accelerated. No amount of looking around the small room produced her.

"When we arrived home, they were missing." Mr. Adelaide ran a hand through his thinning hair as he clutched his wife to his side with the other.

"Mr. Ansley!" Carmichael's shout cut through the tension.

Without excusing himself, Geoffrey fled the room with Elinor's family on his heels. Mrs. Adelaide was in a fit of hysterics, sobbing and wringing her hands. Geoffrey ignored her. He had no time or patience. Carmichael rapidly descended the stairs with a slumped Nigel over his shoulder. "Is he alive?"

"He is, but has a good-sized knot on the back of his head. He'll come around soon." When the valet joined Geoffrey on the lower level, Adelaide took Nigel from him.

"Did you locate Elinor?"

"In passing, which is to say I spotted her through a window. She's tied to a tree on the south lawn. However," Carmichael drew him away from the others. "The north side of the house is on fire. We must hurry."

"Where are the servants?"

Mr. Adelaide shrugged. "They ran away when the first window broke. They're all a superstitious lot."

Well, that changed things. There were no hands available to help put out the fires. "Carmichael, please escort the Adelaides to my home through the passageways. See them settled. I'll join you later with Elinor."

"You don't want my help? There are revelers about but none close."

"I'd rather know her family is safe. If they perish, she'll never forgive me or herself." He clasped the valet's shoulder. "Go. Quickly."

Mr. Adelaide nodded. "Seems the best plan at the moment." He slid an arm around his wife. "Mrs. Adelaide is overly distraught. She doesn't have the constitution for all of this."

Geoffrey nodded. He'd accomplish much more without constantly wondering where Elinor's family was. "Thank you for being so amicable." He glanced at his valet. "You're set?"

"Yes, sir. I'll rouse a couple of the footmen to help stand guard once there."

"Excellent idea." He waited only long enough for Carmichael to lead the Adelaides into the parlor and urge them into the passageway before he tore down the corridor, into the drawing room then out the French doors and onto the terrace very much like his own. The scent of burning, charred wood lingered heavy on the air. The sky flickered in violent shades of orange and red. In random piles, possessions burned. Black smoke billowed upward. One fire contained broken pieces of furniture, another clothing, and still another books and paperwork. "Bastards." What sort of madness drove a person to do such a thing?

Geoffrey prowled between the fires. A few willow trees stood near the southern edge of the lawn, twenty feet or so away from the farthest bonfire. Tied to the trunk of one of them was Elinor. With his heart in his throat, he pelted across the lawn.

"Don't come any closer, Mr. Ansley." A hulking man materialized from the shadows near her tree. "Miss Bennett owes me a kiss before I'll let anyone release her."

"And you would be?" Geoffrey narrowed his eyes. He'd seen the man before around town. The bakery perhaps, the morning he'd stopped by and talked with Elinor?

"He's Michael, the constable's son," Elinor interjected. "No matter how many times I've told him I'll never be interested in him as a man, he still keeps on."

Oh bother. She'd already wounded the man's ego, and now he was having his revenge under the guise of stupid Guy Fawke's mischief. "Does your father know you participated in vandalism tonight?" Geoffrey asked.

Michael shook his head. "And he won't know if you keep your mouth shut." He glared. "He says one more slip on my part and he'll ship me to America, make me fend for myself."

Ah, the lad has more bravado than brains. "I don't suppose you know it's frowned upon to take people—especially women—against their will?"

"She wouldn't listen to me otherwise."

Geoffrey snorted. "Yes, it's one of her special talents, but that's beside the point."

Michael waved a hand. "Do you want to be next on the Guys' list of grievances?"

"Is that a threat?" So much time was wasted conversing with this man. Annoyance rose in Geoffrey's chest in a hot wave.

"It is if you think it is." Michael clenched his hands into fists. "I'll best you, and then you'll know who's the better man for Elinor. She doesn't belong with a snob like you."

"Michael, don't be a bigger arse than you can help." Elinor's taunt tickled Geoffrey's sense of humor.

"Yes, Michael, you might want to follow her instructions. She has the tendency to be a grump if her orders are ignored." Geoffrey reached behind him and pulled his pistol from his waistband. "That being said, I'm afraid you have no claim to the woman, my friend, as she's my bride-to-be." His chest tightened. At least he hoped she would still consider his suit. "I'd hate to shoot you, but I will, unless you remove yourself from this property."

The hulking man with the terrible under bite eyed the pistol. "She owes me a kiss. I've been asking for one every day."

"Let me guess, she tells you no every day?"

He glared. "She does, but I'll just keep asking until she agrees."

Geoffrey snorted. "Good luck with that. Miss Bennett is very stubborn, but I'm quite certain you already know that." He turned slightly at the increased crackling of burning wood. "The fire is spreading." He cocked the pistol then trained it more fully on Michael. "Go home before you find yourself in more trouble than you can imagine."

"I want Elinor."

"So do I." Geoffrey leveled the pistol well over Michael's left shoulder. Elinor screamed at him to leave off. Then he fired.

Of course the shot went wide just as he'd planned. He held the other man's wide-eyed gaze. "The next one won't miss. I suggest you get out of here, for I'm a terribly good shot, and the first one was merely a warning. Push me and you can see that firsthand."

"Oh, bloody hell. You men and your fight for power." Elinor tossed her head. "Michael, come over here."

Geoffrey stared at her. "What are you doing?"

"If the great lout wants a kiss in order to get his bloody arse off the property, so be it. I'll kiss him." She strained against her bonds. "This is my only offer. Take it and go."

Before Geoffrey could offer a protest, Michael approached Elinor. With a smug, lopsided grin, he leaned in and placed a brief kiss on her lips.

"I'm not sorry about the fire," he said as he pulled away. "If you had married me when I asked, I could have taken you away from all of this. Now you've paid the price."

"I'm disappointed in you, Michael. My home is burning down because you were jealous and angry." Elinor shook her head and craned her neck so that she stretched as far away from him as she could. "But if you don't leave immediately, I will instruct Mr. Ansley to shoot you, preferably in your prick and stones, then I'll spit on your body as you bleed to death, and I'll laugh."

Michael's smirk became an angry leer. "You are as mad as the rumors say. Rot with him for all I care." He loped away and didn't look back.

"Well," Geoffrey began. He tucked his pistol into his waistband approached Elinor. The bodice of her dress had been torn. It hung at a drunken angle, exposing the curve of one creamy breast to the nipple. Goose flesh decorated her bare arms, for the air was chilly despite the heat of the fires burning nearby. Dark smudges of soot stained her cheeks and her beautiful hair had fallen from its coif. Some of the tresses were snarled in the tree bark. "It would seem that, yet again, I'm playing the knight and rescuing my fair maiden who is in distress." His mind still spun over the quickly unfolding events of the night.

"It would seem so." Her chin trembled. "Will you please release me?"

"In a moment." He crossed his arms over his chest. His pulse hammered in his temples. The stench of burning wood clung to his nostrils. "What's a man to do when the woman he suspects he's fallen tip over tail for keeps landing into scrapes and awkward situations?" At least for the moment the fires weren't threatening their location. With her tied to the tree, he had her undivided attention.

Elinor worried her bottom lip. She raised her gaze to his. Tears shimmered in the depths. "Carry her off into the sunset then make mad, passionate love to her all night long?"

"You, my girl, are adorable." He couldn't help his chuckle even as his cock thickened. "Oh, I intend to thoroughly satisfy you in bed, but first, I need an answer to my question."

"Which inquiry would that be, Mr. Ansley? I've had a trying night and my mind is scattered." A smile curved her lips.

"The only one that matters." He stepped forward, placed his palms on the wide tree trunk at both sides of her head, and pressed his body into her restrained one. With his lips at the shell of her ear, he said, "Please marry me, Elinor. There is nothing else to say." At least there wasn't while standing out on her fire-dotted lawn where anyone could come upon them.

"I will." She moved her head and kissed the underside of his jaw. "I've been an idiot. If I would have answered you earlier, perhaps this stupidity wouldn't have happened." Her voice wavered.

He pulled back only to cup her cheek. "You cannot know that." When he drew the pad of his thumb along her bottom lip and she shuddered, his chest tightened. "I want to take care of you, show you that even though life does bring heartache and trials at times, it can also be wonderful. I want to make you happy. Be mine. We can move far away from Surrey if you'd like. Return to America. Go anywhere, just as long as you're with me." He'd even dip into the money his father left him in order to buy her some sort of jewelry or even property in America. Wouldn't that put the "family" up in arms to know he'd used their coin to purchase an engagement present for a woman reputed to be mad? He snorted with the ridiculousness of it all.

"Silly man, I said I'd marry you. It matters not where we go." She moved her head slightly and sucked this thumb into her mouth.

Heat erupted through his blood each time Elinor swiped her tongue along his digit. He withdrew. "Very well, now let's free you from your bonds. The sooner I can have you into bed, the sooner I can show you exactly what you mean to me." His heart stuttered as he realized he meant every word. Somehow, she'd snuck into his life and had taken up permanent residence within. He couldn't imagine daily living without her.

"I look forward to it."

"As do I." Geoffrey made quick work of the knotted ropes, and when she came away from the tree trunk with a cry of pain, he caught her into his arms, holding her close. "Are you hurt?"

"No, though I did leave a few strands of hair on the tree." She looped her arms around his shoulders then pressed kisses to his neck, his jawline, his cheeks and finally his lips. "Thank you for always rescuing me at the exact moment I need you—physically and otherwise."

"You are quite welcome, and I will continue to do so until you don't require my services of hero any longer." If he was lucky, they'd have a long life together. He claimed her lips in a brief kiss before holding her at arm's length. "Shall we go home?"

"Yes, but what of my family? Where are they?" She clung to his arm as he steered them toward the fields.

"Carmichael escorted them to my house. They should be safe and sound. We'll sort out the mess once the sun comes up."

"But my house..."

"Is merely a structure that can be rebuilt if your uncle desires it. You and your family escaped." As he spoke, a loud crash rent the relative silence. Geoffrey glanced back in time to see the north side of the manor collapse into itself. "Nothing else is as valuable as knowing you're safe." He held her close to his side, content for the time being in the knowledge he'd rescued and won her. There was time enough for everything else later.

Chapter Ten

Elinor sighed as she wiped away the soot and dirt from her face with a small square of linen. Carmichael, Geoffrey's highly capable butler, had whisked her upstairs upon her arrival and had given her a pretty guestroom done in gold and rose. He advised her to refresh herself and relax, brought in a tea tray then left as quickly as he'd arrived. After folding the damp linen square and laying it on the edge of the basin, she removed her soiled and torn dress as well as toed off her muddy slippers. Finally she finger-combed her tangled hair into some semblance of order. Once finished, there was nothing else with which to keep herself busy, so she lounged in her petticoat and stays as she poured a cup of tea.

She'd barely had time to swallow a few sips before a faint knock sounded and the door swung quietly inward. Geoffrey stood in the frame with a finger to his lips, beckoning to her with his free hand. Intrigued, yet with shivers playing up and down her spine, she followed him, barely aware she still held the teacup. He paused long enough to close the door without a sound then led her down the darkened corridor past several closed doors and finally, at the very end of the hall, he opened yet another door and let her precede him into the room before following and closing that door just as silently.

"Why all the secrecy?" Her pulse fluttered as she caught sight of his familiar four-poster bed and the inside of his bedroom. The low flame from an oil lamp flickered and sent elongated shadows dancing across the hardwood floor. "It feels much different coming into your room from this side of the door."

"Well, that is how proper people enter." Sometime during the night, he'd removed his tailcoat as well as his waistcoat, and she heartily approved. He looked very dashing in his loose-flowing white shirt and dark evening trousers.

"Yet I'm not proper at all." A seed of doubt sprouted deep in her stomach, but died an early death at the heat in his green gaze.

"Thank heavens for that. How boring life would be if everyone in it were proper." He eased the teacup from her fingers then set it down on the bureau top. "Your aunt and uncle have rooms across from yours, as does Nigel. All of them are bruised but none the worse for wear, although your uncle is beside himself from the loss of the manor house."

"I don't understand why we were targeted." She didn't want to think about the burned house or the loss of everything in it. "Michael didn't mean to cause much harm."

"My valet has had word from neighboring estates that mischief and terror were enacted all over Guildford this night. So now, it wasn't just Michael indulging in mischief, but it is troubling. The constable will be here in the morning to take statements."

"How terrible. Why would someone want to destroy property?" Anxiety swirled in her stomach. "I have no more clothes, and of course the passageway is destroyed." She smiled. "That is indeed a shame."

"We no longer have cause to use the passageway any longer. You'll not have a need to spy on me again. I'm at your disposal."

Butterflies took up space in her belly. "True." But had it not been for the passageway, she would never have known Geoffrey in a carnal way. "I must confess I'm a bit sad about that."

"I'm not. I'm glad you won't lurk about in moldy, old corridors any longer. Also, I will be more than happy to provide you with new clothing. Are you certain you're unhurt?" He closed the short distance between them and caressed his fingers over her cheeks then down her back. Awareness trailed in his wake.

"I am fine. Stop fussing." She tried to bat his hands away, but he evaded her protests.

"In this moment, I want to fuss. When my bride-to-be is threatened, the first thing I need to assure myself of is her safety."

"It's different, this relying on another person, trusting someone, with my very being." She swallowed, but the wad of unshed tears in her throat wouldn't dislodge. "When my parents died and then my brother, I felt so alone. I didn't know if I'd ever be able to let someone close to me again."

"And now?" He hadn't touched her yet, almost as if he didn't trust himself to move.

"Now," her chin quivered. A tear splashed onto her cheek. "I not only trust but, but I also have the urge to let you fully into my life and tell you everything about me, share my hopes and dreams." Another tear fell. "What does that mean?"

"Oh, my dear." Geoffrey caught her hands in his. "It means you've been left to your own devices for far too long. I intend to be everything you need, provide comfort and understanding when appropriate and love you when everything else doesn't work."

Her heart trembled. "Oh Geoffrey." How long had she wished for someone to do just that? Ever since she'd lost her parents and had felt out to sea. "It all sounds so wonderful."

He drew one of her hands to his lips and kissed the back of it. "I'm only that way when you're by my side. You make me a better man."

Another few tears fell to her cheeks. Elinor had no idea how she came to be so lucky. A week ago, she'd been teetering on the cusp of despair at the hole in her life. Now, she was engaged to be married, and her fiancé was nothing short of wonderful. Who knew spying on a man while he sat in a bathtub would lead to so much joy? "Thank you for saving me... in more ways than one." A fresh torrent fell. "I don't know that I deserve such interest. What if you change your mind, or find I'm not what you're looking for in a wife, or I'm—"

"Hush, my love." He pressed a kiss to her forehead. The scents of charred wood and the out of doors clung to his clothes. "I've never been so certain of anything. My mind is quite firmly made up." Other kisses followed to her cheeks, her chin, the tip of her nose. He kissed away her tears and left nothing but gladness behind. "I'm mad about you, Elinor. I don't know how or when it happened, but it has, and I couldn't be happier."

"We cannot both be mad, Geoffrey. What will everyone say?" Unable to let him have all the enjoyment, she followed his lead and trailed her lips along the underside of his jaw, down the strong column of his throat then nipped the skin over his Adam's apple. When he uttered a sharp hiss, she grinned and licked her lips. Salty sweat clung to them.

"Outside of congratulations on our upcoming nuptials, I don't care what anyone says regarding you and I."

She worried her bottom lip. "What if...?"

"Don't even think about things that haven't happened or may not happen." He kissed her, catching her bottom lip between his teeth and lightly biting. "Sometimes life will hurt, but there will also be glorious moments. Live for those moments, with me. Together, we'll meet every challenge and be the stronger for it."

"I will." Her chin trembled. "Don't ever leave me, Geoffrey."

"I have no plans to do so." He grabbed handfuls of her petticoat and drew it up her body then off altogether. Dropping it onto the floor, he said, "I propose we continue this discussion in the bed since I plan to make... what was it you asked of me? Mad, passionate love to you all night long?"

Her face warmed. The tight buds of her sensitized nipples scraped against the cotton shift she still wore. Oh, how she wanted him. "Yes." She tugged the ends of his shirt from his trousers then slid her hands up his hard chest. "I would like to start as soon as we can."

"As would I." Emotion graveled his voice, but she could only read shadows in his eyes. "Turn." He spun her around. Seconds later, he plucked at the laces of her stays. They fell away in short order. "I adore assisting you out of your clothes." Geoffrey tugged off her shift and it dropped to the floor with a whisper. "Once we're wed, you and I aren't leaving a bedroom for days."

"Perhaps we should start marking time now." Elinor shivered as he cupped her breasts from behind. "Mmm." She pressed his hands tighter against her bosom. "I need you to touch me here."

"I plan to touch every inch of your skin tonight and then some." When he rubbed his palms over her distended nipples, she moaned.

Tingles erupted between her breasts then zipped along an invisible cord to her core. "More. You make me feel like flying." She whimpered as he rolled the aching buds. The whimpers became pants of need when he pinched them. "Oh, please more." Pleasure-tipped pain flooded her.

"That's what I what to hear." His whisper warmed her ear, and his solid body pressed against her backside sent fires along her skin. "Now I *will* make you fly."

Her breathing intensified, even more so as he slid a hand down her body, past the soft swell of her belly then pushed onward. His fingers slipped through the curls shrouding her mound. With his index finger and thumb, he parted her lower lips.

"Spread your legs, Elinor. Let me play." He followed the command with a nip to her earlobe and a pinch to her nipple.

When she did as instructed, Geoffrey moved his hand between her thighs. Again and again, he strummed his fingers along her folds, and each time collected the moisture escaping her passage, slickening the sensitize skin of her sex. "Geoffrey, please." She pressed his hand tighter to her mound, but he wouldn't rush. "Impossible man."

"You have no idea." He nipped her lobe again at the same time he penetrated her pulsing channel with one long finger. "I love how hot, how wet, how tight you are."

She couldn't answer, not when he added a second finger. Once he found a rhythm, thrusting with first a long stroke followed by two short ones, her brain ceased to function. Elinor lifted a hand to wrap her fingers around his nape in an effort to stay upright. Then his strokes changed, and he explored, pressing them against a certain spot deep inside that wrenched a surprised moan from her throat each time he brushed it.

"I fear I'll break apart."

"That's the point, my love." He massaged the spot again then added his thumb to the torture cycle. Over and over, he brought his drenched fingers out of her passage and circled her swollen numb then he returned them to her core, plunging in and out. "Fly for me. Come apart in my arms so I can make love to you with my cock." He fluttered his fingers deep inside, and the sensations of bliss that welled up from the action almost melted her knees.

Elinor shook from his words, his fingers, and the images that sprang into her mind. Having his hand between her legs was ever so much better than pleasuring herself. She circled an aching nipple with her free hand, brushing her fingers over the hard tip in time to his torment of her slick flesh. Bands of pressure built and stacked within. They circled inside like a hungry beast intent on devouring her whole until she couldn't hold it back any longer. When she pinched her nipple and plucked it, he did the same with her swollen button.

Then she shattered. A soft cry left her throat as waves of pleasure broke over her. They tickled along her skin and warmed her limbs while her inner walls squeezed around his fingers. Her legs no longer supported her weight, and when she slumped against the hard wall of his body, he caught her with an arm around her waist.

"Now that you're relaxed, it's time to move to the bed." Half-carrying and half-walking with her, Geoffrey led her to that piece of furniture then helped her onto it. "I'll be with you in a trifle, my girl."

In a daze she lay back against the mound of pillows. The comforter smelled like him, so clean and with a hint of spices. Tiny tremors danced through her body as she watched him undress. He was unlike any other man she'd ever known, and so caring and considerate she wanted to cry from happiness. But she didn't. She couldn't. The only thing she did was grin a fool's grin as his shirt hit the floor, closely followed by his trousers, and when he was as gloriously naked as she, she explored him with her hungry gaze.

Every ridge, dip, and plain over his abdomen and chest was contoured with shadow from the oil lamp. Blond hair lay sprinkled over his pectoral muscles. It culminated in a thin ribbon that played over his abdomen and ended in a light nest at the base of his cock.

Elinor licked her lips in anticipation. Would he let her pleasure him with her mouth tonight? "I cannot believe you chose me," she whispered as he prowled across the room with a glint of wicked intent in his eyes.

"How could I not when you enchanted me from the first?" Geoffrey joined her on the bed, kneeling between her spread legs. "Since your naughty little secret was what brought us together, perhaps you should do so for my pleasure tonight."

Her breath caught. "You wish for me to do that while you watch?" The very idea left her both hot and cold at the same time.

"It would only be fair." He drew his gaze down her body, lingered on the wet flesh between her thighs before returning it to hers once more.

"I suppose I could." Elinor furrowed her fingers through the damp curls covering her mound until she found her swollen button. A tiny gasp escaped her throat. The familiar bands of need pulled tight deep inside. "Though I'd much rather find release from your cock instead."

"Perhaps we should save that exhibition for another time." He pounced, partially covering her body with him. "I felt a pull since we sat in that parlor and you told me about your family. I wanted to see you smile, needed to make you see that happiness is all around us if we would just acknowledge it."

She held his dear face between her hands and peered into his eyes. "I'll try to be everything you want."

"No." He dipped his head and brushed his lips over hers. "You are already everything I want. Don't change who you are for an ideal of who you think I need."

"And no matter what, you'll support me, even if I want to continue to work in the bakery?" The hot, thickness of his engorged length rested against her thigh, and she squirmed, hoping to urge him to where she needed him to be.

"My girl, if you decide you want to sit in the village square and sing lullabies, I won't dissuade you. I'll merely stand at your side and defend you against the rumormongers. I'll tell the world how clever I think you are, because nothing else matters. I've won you." He slid a hand between their bodies then brushed his fingers along her swollen button. "Please tell me you're ready for me." Passion roughened his voice. "I adore conversing with you, but I'd rather love you at the moment."

Her heart quaked. An answering throb rocked her core. She wriggled beneath him, and the wide tip of his length brushed her opening. Her breath caught. The moment just before joining was one of her most favorite. "Yes, please."

Then she was lost on a sea of feeling as he took his weight on his forearms and flexed his hips. His cock slid easily into her passage, and he didn't stop the push until he was completely seated.

"I adore this moment." The feeling of fullness, of being one with the man she was beginning to love beyond distraction tickled her heart and brought tears to her eyes. Physical relations were so much more meaningful when her heart and emotions were involved. The act went beyond the physical and touched her soul, leaving her whole again. "I love you."

Geoffrey's eyes widened and he stilled with his forehead resting on hers. "Truly?"

"Yes." She hugged him close. "I only just realized it, and I don't care if it sounds silly or is too soon, or—"

He cut her off with a quick kiss. "I love you too." Then he moved his hips and his cock slid free. "We're going to have a delightful time together."

Elinor didn't answer with words. She couldn't, not when tears of joy crowded into her throat. Instead, she lifted her legs and locked her ankles behind his back. When he moved within her, she tilted her hips and met each thrust. He drove deep with every penetration. Harder and harder, each breach rubbed the base of his length over her sensitive nub and loosed hosts of hot tingles throughout her body.

"Geoffrey, yes, more." She rocked in time to his strokes, and then on one particularly enthusiastic thrust, her world exploded. Pressure broke, and the force of her release gripped every point of her body. She tightly closed her eyes and dug her fingernails into his upper arms. Pleasure swamped every inch of her, even curled her toes as her inner walls fluttered around his pulsing cock.

He shoved inside once more, uttering a sharp gasp and grinding his pelvis into hers. "Good God, woman, you wear me out." Once he collapsed to one side of her, he pulled her back against his front. "And I adore you."

His voice rumbled in her ear, and she snuggled even closer to him. "Next time, I intend to ride you. I've always wanted to try that position."

"Let me nap for an hour. Then I'll indulge you in whatever you want." Geoffrey wrapped his arms around her, and she covered his arms with hers. "Where should we start our wedding trip?"

Elinor's mind spun with the possibilities, but in his arms, she felt safe and needed for the first time in many years. "I say we start it right here in this bed. Then we'll decide where to go after that."

"I like the way you think." He heaved a sigh which turned into a yawn. "I'm so glad I came to Surrey. It's proved to be the best thing that has ever happened to me."

The tears that had been threatening since he'd freed her from the tree fell to wet her cheeks. She clutched one of his hands then kissed his palm. "I agree." Elinor snuggled closer and found a more comfortable position on the pillows.

Finally, the gaping emptiness she'd carried around since she'd lost her family was filled with Geoffrey's love, and returning the emotion, while terrifying in its vastness and its unknown, smoothed out the rough edges. Life was full of new experiences, and the learning of each would make her a stronger person regardless of the outcome.

She couldn't wait to begin the journey with him.

The End

To find out what happens next to Elinor and Geoffrey, read A Garden Affair

(Scandalous Short #4)

Elinor Bennett's days of spying on her handsome neighbor—now husband—might be over, but her penchant for watching him is still her favorite hobby, especially when he's *sans* clothing. Yet some of the illicit excitement she felt during the early days of courtship have faded. How to rekindle that spark?

Geoffrey has been kept busy with solicitor work for the village he's adopted, but time between the sheets with his new bride is at a premium. He remembers their scandalous past fondly and though he and Elinor had made bed sport wicked then, would she still want the same now that she was respectably wed?

Imagine Elinor's surprise when she peeps on her husband in the garden and finds him completely naked and very much aroused. Sexual games abound amidst the fragrant blooms and as passion erupts into glorious color, a new aspect to their relationship is revealed.

Warning: at 5K words, this is a short story. For longer novels, please browse the *Scandal in Surrey* collection. To find out how the romance began, purchase *Miss Bennett's Naughty Secret*.

Regency-era romances by Sandra Sookoo

Colors of Scandal series
Dressed in White
Draped in Green
Trimmed in Blue
Wrapped in Red
Graced in Scarlet
Adorned in Violet
Embellished in Mauve
Clad in Midnight
Garbed in Purple
Resplendent in Ruby
Cloaked in Shadows
Decorated in Christmas
Tangled in Lavender
Persuasive in Pink
Disguised in Tartan (coming April 2022)
Attired in Highland Gold (coming April 2022)
Hopeful in Yellow (coming August 2022)
Imperfect in Peridot (coming October 2022)
Christmas in Crimson (coming November 2022)
Storme Brothers series
The Soul of a Storme
The Heart of a Storme
The Look of a Storme
A Storme's Christmas Legacy
A Storme's First Noelle (in the *Star of Light* anthology)
The Sting of a Storme
The Touch of a Storme
The Fury of a Storme (coming May 2022)
Home for the Holidays series
The Folly of Caroling

Three Mistletoe Kisses
Silver Bells Scandal
A Holly and Ivy Affair
Lords of the Night series
Devil Take the Duke
Bitten by the Earl
Adrift with the Viscount
Treasured by the Earl
Transformed by a Christmas Star
Pistols at Dawn, Your Grace, as part of the *Shifting Hearts* boxed set
Willful Winterbournes series
Romancing Miss Quill (coming June 2022)
Pursuing Mr. Mattingly (coming August 2022)
Courting Lady Yeardly (coming October 2022)
Teasing Miss Atherby (coming late 2022 or early 2023?)
Singular Sensation series
One Little Indiscretion (coming July 2022)
One Secret Wish (coming September 2022)
One Tiny On-Dit Later (coming January 2023)
One Accidental Night with an Improper Duke (coming March 2023)
One Scandalous Choice (coming May 2023)
One Thing Led to Another (coming July 2023)
One Too Many Suitors (coming September 2023)
One Thing Led to Another (November 2023)
Mary and Bright series
A Mary and Bright Christmastide (coming December 2023)
A Springtime Engagement (TBA)
An Autumnal Partnership (TBA)
Diamonds of London series
My Dear Mr. Ridley (coming February 14, 2023)
The Clever Widow's Wager (coming April 23, 2023)
Catch Her if You Can (coming June 13, 2023)
Yours Respectfully, My Lord (coming August 15, 2023)
When the Duke Said Yes (coming September 14, 2023)
To Love a Ghostly Lord (coming October 17, 2023)
One Hell of a Christmas (coming November 20, 2023)

Along Came Tess (coming January 16, 2024)
The Duke's Valentine (coming February 13, 2024
Not in His Usual Style (coming March 12, 2024)
The Merry Month of May (coming April 16, 2024)
The Duchess Problem (coming May 14, 2024)
Spirited Away by the Viscount (June 11, 2024)

Thieves of the Ton series
Captivated by an Adventurous Lady
Engaged to a Scandalous Earl
Married on a Wicked Morning
Intrigued by an Ancient Pedigree
Beguiled on a Christmas Morning: Christmas novella
Caught with a Stolen Diamond
Tortured by a Horrible Secret
Delighted on a Summer's Evening
Trapped in the British Museum
Charmed at a Yuletide Ball
One Silent Night
Redeeming a Tarnished Lord
Lords of Happenstance series
What the Stubborn Viscount Desires
What a Wayward Lord Needs
What the Dashing Duke Deserves
Scandal in Surrey series
Lady Parker's Grand Affair
The Bride's Gambit
Misfortune's Lady
Miss Bennett's Naughty Secret
Standalone Regency romances
Lady Isabella's Splendid Folly
Wagering on Christmas
Magic in Mayflowers
Act of Pardon

Angel's Master
Storm Tossed Rogue
Claiming His Wife
Scoundrel's Trespass
On a Midnight Clear
A Fowl Christmastide
His Pretend Duchess
Visions of Christmastide
An Accidental Countess
A Rogue for Lady Peacock (coming September 2022)
The Most Wonderful Earl of the Year (coming November 2022)
Snowflakes for the Earl (coming December 2022)
She's Got a Duke to Keep Her Warm (coming December 2022)
The Most Wonderful Earl of the Year (coming December 2022)
The Lyon's Dilemma (Lyon's Den connected world) (coming January 2023)

Author Bio

Sandra Sookoo is a *USA Today* bestselling author who firmly believes every person deserves acceptance and a happy ending. Most days you can find her creating scandal and mischief in the Regency-era, serendipity and happenstance in Victorian America or snarky, sweet humor in the contemporary world. Most recently she's moved into infusing her books with mystery and intrigue. Reading is a lot like eating fine chocolates—you can't just have one. Good thing books don't have calories!

When she's not wearing out computer keyboards, Sandra spends time with her real-life Prince Charming in central Indiana where she's been known to goof off and make moments count because the key to life is laughter. A Disney fan since the age of ten, when her soul gets bogged down and her imagination flags, a trip to Walt Disney World is in order. Nothing fuels her dreams more than the land of eternal happy endings, hope and love stories.

Stay in Touch

Sign up for Sandra's bi-monthly newsletter and you'll be given exclusive excerpts, cover reveals before the general public as well as opportunities to enter contests you won't find anywhere else.

Just send an email to sandrasookoo@yahoo.com with SUBSCRIBE in the subject line.

Or follow/friend her on social media:

Facebook: https://www.facebook.com/sandra.sookoo

Facebook Author Page: https://www.facebook.com/sandrasookooauthor/

Pinterest: https://www.pinterest.com/sandrasookoo/

Instagram: https://www.instagram.com/sandrasookoo/

BookBub Page: https://www.bookbub.com/authors/sandra-sookoo

Don't miss out!

Visit the website below and you can sign up to receive emails whenever Sandra Sookoo publishes a new book. There's no charge and no obligation.

https://books2read.com/r/B-A-PDBB-KZXE

Connecting independent readers to independent writers.